TRIUMPH
ENTERTAINMENT

WHAT'S INSIDE!

Winning Decks

Card Collection Tips

Top TEN Cards in Each Series

Gen Con Indy

Naruto Puzzles

the WHO'S WHO of NARUTO!

Do you know your Itachi
from your Sakura?
Well, this bio guide
Will bring you up to speed on
all of Naruto's main players!

Naruto Uzumaki

Naruto is the main character of the show. He is an outgoing ninja who's prime goal is to become the **Kage** of his village - **The Village Hidden in the Leaves.** Naruto is very different compared to other ninjas his age. He doesn't have any special bloodline powers, but was born with the power of the **nine-tailed demon fox sealed** inside of his body. Long ago this demon fox terrorized the Village Hidden in the Leaves causing catastrophic damage. In order to save the village, **The Third Hokage** had to perform a forbidden jutsu to seal the powers of this demon fox inside Naruto. This caused the Third Hokage to lose his own life. The Third Hokage's hope was that one day people would consider Naruto a hero for saving the village from complete destruction.

Naruto's Biography Continued

Instead of considering Naruto a hero, many villagers consider him to be the reincarnation of the demon fox and therefore shun him. Naruto, who is an orphan, is lonely throughout most of his childhood. He counters being ignored by pulling pranks around the village to get attention. Despite being quite the prankster and pest, Naruto has a very likable personality. He always tries his hardest to accomplish things even when they seem too tough. Naruto's determination inspires many other ninjas to realize their own goals.

One of the challenges Naruto faces throughout the show is his ability to control the power of the demon fox inside of his body. The demon fox's powers are so immense that if it isn't controlled correctly, it can severely hurt or even kill Naruto. One special power of the demon fox is the fact that it can heal open wounds on Naruto's body. The powers of the demon fox, when tapped into, are visible by an **orange aura** *that surrounds Naruto's body. Oftentimes, the powers of the demon fox are unleashed when Naruto is extremely angry. The demon fox plays a very important part in the series as criminals are out to capture it's immense power.*

Naruto is part of the Village Hidden in the Leave's **Genin Team 7**, *which consists of* **Naruto, Sasuke, and Sakura.** *Kakashi is their assigned team leader. Naruto and Sasuke have a very unique relationship. Sasuke is, in essence, the anti-Naruto. Sasuke keeps to himself and is liked by all the girls, while Naruto is seen as loud and obnoxious. They struggle to get along early but later on develop a close relationship even though sometimes it doesn't seem so. Naruto has a secret crush on Sakura, however, Sakura usually ignores Naruto and finds him annoying.*

Sakura Haruno

Sakura is the only girl in **Team 7**. Early on, Sakura is pretty much obsessed with Sasuke, always giving him compliments and trying to be near him. She even grows out her hair because she hears from someone that Sasuke likes girls with long hair.

Sakura would completely tune out Naruto because she thought of him as annoying. However as the series progresses, Sakura starts to become closer to Naruto and appreciate him more for his dedication and tenacity.

Unlike the other 2 ninjas on her team, Sakura wasn't born with any special abilities. Being a girl, she has a much smaller amount of **chakra** available to her. However, one special thing about Sakura is her ability to efficiently use and control her chakra, as stated by Kakashi.

It is not until later on, when she trains with Tsunade, that Sakura is able to tap into her great ability of controlling chakra. After training with Tsunade, Sakura becomes extremely skilled at healing wounds.

She becomes the medical ninja of her team. Much of Sakura's skill comes from her ability to heal injured ninjas in a very timely manner. Sakura is also able to build up chakra on her fists, making them extremely powerful. Much of Sakura's fighting involves straight punching.

Sasuke is another ninja that belongs to **Team 7**. Unlike Naruto, Sasuke has a quiet demeanor. He doesn't show many emotions at all. Many of the girls in the **Village Hidden in the Leaf** think Sasuke is cute, such as Sakura, but he usually doesn't acknowledge it. To a certain extent, it seems that he really doesn't care for any of his teammates. Sasuke feels that Naruto and Sakura are nothing but deterrence to his goal of killing his bother. He is a loner by nature ever since a terrible event occurred during his childhood.

Sasuke is part of a very prestigious clan, the **Uchiha**. One day as a child, Sasuke comes home to find his whole clan completely wiped out. He sees his brother Itachi standing over the dead bodies claiming he killed the clan simply to see his own strength.

Sasuke Uchiha

Itachi also tells Sasuke that he never loved him and that he wasn't even worth killing. Ever since that day, Sasuke has dedicated his life to one day get strong enough to take down his brother. He hopes that by taking out his brother, he can get revenge for all of the other clan members and also bring the clan back to greatness.

The **Uchiha** members have a special ability known as the Sharingan. This ability was not given to Sasuke at birth, but activated during a battle at some point in during his chidlhood. The Sharingan can be distinguished by **red eyes with black markings on it.** This bloodline is extremely powerful because it allows Sasuke to track things going very fast and also see through **Genjutsu, Taijutsu, and Ninjutsu attacks.** As the Sharingan is perfected, it also allows Sasuke to cast illusions to confuse his opponents. The Sharingan plays a major role in Sasuke's growth as a ninja and in fighting his brother.

Kakashi Hatake

Kakashi is a **Jonin ranked ninja** and also the leader of **Team 7**. He was also formerly part of the **ANBU squad**. Unlike most team leaders, Kakashi is pretty laid back. He goes about things nonchalantly, often times even arriving late on days of missions. However, don't let his behavior fool you. When it comes to a serious situation, Kakashi is always ready and prepared. Kakashi's closest friend in the show is Might Guy, another instructor. Kakashi and Might have a very intense rivalry consisting of actual battles and rounds of rock-paper-scissors.

Though not being from the **Uchiha clan**, Kakashi has the special **Sharingan power**. Kakashi acquired the Sharingan through a surgical procedure early on from one of his closest friends Obito Uchiha, who died in battle. Because he is not a natural carrier of the Sharingan, it takes a lot more chakra and energy for him to use it. This is why Kakashi usually has the eye which he carries the Sharingan on covered. This way it doesn't tire out. Kakashi is known as the **"Copy Ninja"** because of his mastery of the Sharingan. It has been said that he has copied over 1000 jutsus.

One of Kakashi's hobbies, which he keeps hidden from his students and ninjas, is reading the **Come Come Paradise**, which details the love life of Jiraiya. Kakashi throughout the series is completely infatuated with the book, always eagerly awaiting the next edition.

Rock Lee

Rock Lee is known as a ninja that specializes in **Taijutsu (hand to hand combat).** Rock Lee is physically incapable of performing any **Genjutsu or Ninjutsu.** This handicap forced him to specialize solely on Taijutsu. He is part of **Team Guy,** which is led by Might Guy. Guy takes a special interest in Rock Lee because he sees all of the dedication he has to put in to overcome his shortcomings. They have a very strong bond, almost like a father-son relationship.

Physically, Rock Lee looks very similar to Might Guy. They both have their signature bowl-cut hairstyles, thick eyebrows, and they wear green jumpsuits. Rock Lee is very respectful to everyone. He doesn't hold grudges and always sees things in a positive way.

Might Guy

Guy is the leader of **Team Guy**, which consists of Rock Lee, Neji Hyuga, and Tenten. Guy looks pretty much like an older Rock Lee. He has a bowl cut, thick eyebrows, and always wears a green jumpsuit. One difference between the two is that Guy also wears a green vest. Guy likes to fight with mostly physical attacks. Unlike Lee, who is incapable of doing anything else, Guy simply just chooses to fight this way because of personal preference.

Might Guy has a very passionate personality. He is very strict on Rock Lee, who he takes under his wing. Guy claims Kakashi to be his rival, though the rivalry seems one-sided most of the time because of Kakashi's nonchalant attitude.

POJO'S UNOFFICIAL TOTAL NARUTO!

Gaara comes from the **Village Hidden in the Sand**. He is a youngest of three siblings. He has a sister named Temari and a brother named Kankuro. Gaara is the son of the Kazekage.

Gaara was born with the powers of the **One-Tailed Shukaku** sealed within himself. This was done by his father hoping to make him a very strong military weapon. But due to Gaara's instability, his father tried to have him murdered. The murder backfired and

Gaara became very emotionally unstable.

In a way Gaara can relate to Naruto because they both have demons sealed within their bodies. People from their respective villages considered them to be inhuman.

Gaara has a **red marking** on the side of the forehead which says **"Love"**. The lettering reminds him only to love

himself and fight for himself. However, as the show progresses, Gaara's attitude changes and when he sees how Naruto cares for him.

Gaara

Neji Hyuga

Neji is part of the **lower class of the Hyugan Clan**. Being part of the lower branch, his sole duty was to protect the main family. There is a mark on Neji's forehead that allows the main family to mess with Neji's mind. Neji has a very strong hatred towards his clan because of the fact that his father was sacrificed. It later turns out his father had volunteered himself to protect the family and also pave the way for others, including Neji, to choose their own paths in life and not always follow tradition.

He has a special bloodline power in his eyes called the **Byakugan**. This special power allows him to see in all directions and also critical areas where chakra flows in a person's body.

POJO'S UNOFFICIAL TOTAL NARUTO!

Shikamaru

Shikamaru is part of **Team 10** with Choji and Ino. His team leader is Asuma. Shikamaru is known to be extremely lazy. He shows almost no emotions for anything unless there is an extreme need, like when his teammates are in imminent danger. Shikamaru usually spends his free time taking naps and watching clouds opposed to training.

Shikamaru is actually very intelligent despite his laziness. He has an extremely high IQ. The only reason he has such poor grades is his refusal to do any work. When Shikamaru is in battle, he usually uses his **Shadow Imitation jutsu**. This technique allows him to capture the shadow of his opponent, preventing his opponent from moving.

Akimichi Choji

Choji is another member of **Team 10**. He considers Shikamaru to be his best friend. Choji is extremely fat, though he likes to deny it. He is always eating. One special ability that Choji has is his ability to exponentially increase his size. This is a special power the people of his clan have.

Shino Aburame

Shino is part of **Team 8,** which is led by Kurenai Yuhi. Shino has an extreme fascination with insects. He is always looking and examining new ones. Shino comes from the **Aburame clan,** which is a clan that has a special connection with insects. Every clan member born has special destructive insects that infest over his or her body. These bugs live in Shino's body and survive on his chakra. In exchange for living on his body, the bugs do as Shino wants. He usually uses these bugs to fight his opponents.

Hinata Hyuga

Hinata is the heiress of the **Hyuga Clan**. She is Neji's cousin. However, she was disowned by her father at a young age because of her inability to speak up and stand up for herself. She suffers from lack of self confidence.

Hinata was taken in by Kurenai at a young age and is part of **Team 8.** Hinata mainly trains to prove to her father that she is worthy of being a Hyuga. Hinata has a secret crush on Naruto throughout the show. She always blushes around him. However, she is afraid to tell Naruto of her true feelings.

Jiraiya

Jiraiya is one of the **three Legendary Sannin**. He is also called the **Toad Sage** because many of his techniques involve the usage of toads. Jiraiya is one of Naruto's teachers. He is an extremely skilled fighter and was trained by the Third Hokage. Jiraiya has a very interesting personality. He is infatuated with women. He is always staring at women and is the author of a romance novel series.

Zabuza Momochi

Zabuza is one of the first villains Naruto faces. He is from the **Village Hidden in the Mist**. Zabuza was one of the **Seven Swordsmen from the Mist Village**. After failing to kill the leader of the Mist Village, Zabuza fled the village and became a hired assassin. He wields a very large sword that is as big as his body.

Zabuza is hired to kill a man named Tazuna, but is stopped by Kakashi and Team 7. Zabuza's employer is disappointed that Zabuza is having difficulty completing the task, and tries to have Zabuza killed. Zabuza kills his employer, but dies in the process. (See Page 37 for more details).

Haku

Haku is an orphan that is taken in by **Zabuza** at a very young age. He is very attached to Zabuza and actually gives his life away to save Zabuza from **Kakashi**. Haku has a special bloodline ability that involves the skill to manipulate ice. He is known to send out mirrors of ice to surround the opponent, then attack opponents with ice needles.

Orochimaru

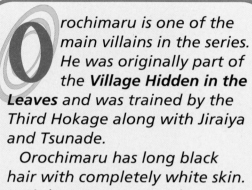rochimaru is one of the main villains in the series. He was originally part of the **Village Hidden in the Leaves** and was trained by the Third Hokage along with Jiraiya and Tsunade.

Orochimaru has long black hair with completely white skin. He is known to use snakes and serpents in many of his attacks. He has many similar characteristics as a snake such as having a very long tongue that he sometimes uses to fight.

Orochimaru fled his village and eventually joined the Akatsuki. Orochimaru eventually left the Akatsuki after an incident and set out to destroy the **Village Hidden in the Leaves**.

POJO'S UNOFFICIAL TOTAL NARUTO!

Kiba Inuzuka

Kiba is part of **Team 8** along with Shino and Hinata. He is from the **Inuzaka Clan**, which has a very strong connection with canines. Kiba is rarely found without his dog **Akamaru**.

Kiba has many similar characteristics as a canine. When Kiba fights, he usually gets on all fours, similar to a dog. He also has a very strong sense of smell, which becomes useful for tracking down opponents.

Kurenai Yuhi

Kurenai is the leader of **Team 8**. She has a very strong relationship with Hinata primarily because of how Hinata was disowned by her father. Kurenai uses illusionary techniques when she fights, most of the time involving plants. She is usually seen together with Asuma, though it is unconfirmed that they are a couple.

POJO'S UNOFFICIAL TOTAL NARUTO!

Ino Yamanaka

Ino is part of **Team 10** with Shikamaru and Choji. She and Sakura are childhood friends and both have crushes on Sasuke. When they found out that they each liked Sasuke, their friendship ended and they ended up competing with each other to try to impress him. Eventually they settled their differences, but they still are very competitive with each other. Ino specializes in mind altering jutsus, which allows her to control the body of her opponents. She also learns to become a **medical ninja** from Sakura.

Asuma Sarutobi

Asuma is the son of the Third Hokage and the leader of **Team 10**. Asuma has a close relationship with Shikamaru. When he fights, he usually wears **brass knuckles** filled with chakra transferred from his body. Asuma eventually is killed by one of the members of the Akatsuki, but his death is avenged by Shikamaru.

Tenten

Tenten is an extremely skilled female ninja who is part of **Team Guy**. As a child, she idolized Tsunade. She has a very strong relationship with Neji, someone she respects highly. Many times she helps train Neji to get him stronger. Tenten specializes in using weapons when she fights. She has the ability to summon hundreds of weapons at a time to attack her opponents.

Kankuro

Kankuro is from the **Village Hidden in the Sand** and is Gaara's brother. Early on, Kankuro was very afraid of Gaara and his instability. As the series progressed, the two developed a closer bond. Kankuro is known to fight with puppets. He has three specific puppets he uses, all created by the legendary **Sasori**.

Temari

Temari is Gaara's sister and also from the **Village Hidden in the Sand**. Temari is almost like a peacemaker, always trying to find a way to solve things without violence. When she does fight, she uses a large fan that can create huge gusts of wind.

Iruka Umino

Iruka is an instructor in the **Ninja Academy**. In the very beginning of the show, Iruka is saved by Naruto, and because of this, he allows Naruto to graduate. Iruka's parents were killed by the demon fox sealed inside Naruto. However, he doesn't have any bad feelings towards Naruto. Instead, he is one of the few people that understand it is not Naruto's fault and treats Naruto as just a normal human being. Iruka is almost like a father figure to Naruto.

Konohamaru

Konohamaru is the grandson of the Third Hokage. He is very young and still in the academy. Konohamaru looks up to Naruto and hopes one day to become Hokage, only after Naruto becomes Hokage.

Sarutobi
The Third Hokage

Sarutobi is the Third Hokage and also the longest reigning Hokage. He assumed his duties back after the death of the Fourth Hokage. Sarutobi is very wise and is always looking to instill his wisdom on the younger generation. He believes in peace and harmony more than anything else. Sarutobi trained Jiraiya, Tsunade, and Orochimaru. Eventually he gives his life away to stop Orochimaru from destroying the village.

POJO'S UNOFFICIAL TOTAL NARUTO!
This book is not sponsored, endorsed by, or otherwise affiliated with any of the companies or products featured in this book.
This is not an official publication.

Tsunade
The Fifth Hokage

Tsunade is the Fifth Hokage, taking over after Sarutobi passed away. She is the granddaughter of the First Hokage. Tsunade has a very bad gambling problem that loses her a lot of money.

Tsunade is an amazing medical ninja and also has superhuman strength. She takes Sakura under her wing and teaches her medical skills. Just like the other 2 of the Legendary Sannin, Tsunade has a special connection with an animal. She has the ability to summon **slugs** to fight.

Kisame is a member of the Akatsuki. He is one of the **Seven Swordsman** like Zabuza. Kisame somewhat resembles a shark with his pale skin, sharp teeth, and gills over his face. He wields a very large sword that has scales all over it. This sword allows Kisame to suck the chakra away from his opponents.

Kisame Hoshigaki

Itachi Uchiha

Itachi is a member of the **Akatsuki** and part of the **Uchiha Clan**. He decimated the village leaving his younger brother Sasuke as the only other survivor. Itachi has a very advanced form of the **Sharingan** which makes him very hard to defeat. He has the ability to defeat an opponent without moving at all, simply by trapping them inside illusions. As part of the Akatsuki, he and other members are assigned to obtain the demon sealed inside Naruto and others such as Gaara.

ALL ABOUT NINJAS

Ninja Rankings

Academy Students are usually kids of very young age who hope to one day become a ninja. Academy students do not go on missions but are taught in school many of the basics of being a ninja such as performing basic techniques and skills. In order to become a **Genin** and graduate from the Ninja Academy, the student must pass a special test. This test, however, is not easy. Many students find themselves unable to pass the test.

Genin

Genin is the **lowest rank** for a ninja. Each Genin has a Jonin instructor that helps train the Genin to become a great ninja. Genins are typically not allowed to go on missions but instead train just like students of the Academy. Many times Genins will be assigned to do laboring work. When Genins do go on missions, they are usually put into the lowest mission level, **D.**

POJO'S UNOFFICIAL TOTAL NARUTO!

Chunin

Chunin is the **medium rank** for a ninja. In order to become a Chunin, a Genin must be nominated by their teacher and then pass a special test that tests a ninja's mental and physical strength. Becoming a Chunin is not an easy task as many ninjas have died taking the Chunin Exam. Once a Genin becomes a Chunin, he or she will have a wider range of missions they can perform such as combat and assassination missions.

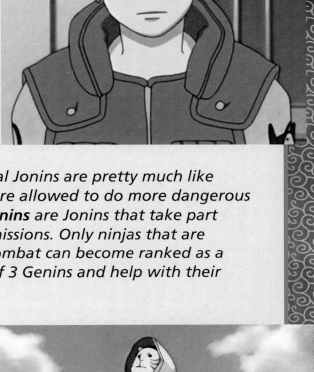

Jonin

Jonin is split into **2 categories.** The next rank up from the Chunin level is **Special Jonin.** Special Jonins are pretty much like Chunins except they are allowed to do more dangerous missions. **Complete Jonins** are Jonins that take part in the most difficult missions. Only ninjas that are extremely skilled in combat can become ranked as a Jonin. Jonins are also required to be the teacher of 3 Genins and help with their development.

ANBU

ANBU is not a real ninja rank, but is a **special group** of ninjas that operate under the command of his or her village's **Kage**. ANBU members wear animal masks that represent animals of the Zodiac. This helps in protecting their identities and also induces fear. ANBU members perform extremely dangerous missions and usually have a really short life expectancy.

Kage

Kage is the **highest rank** for a ninja. Each village has **one** Kage who acts as the village's leader. Usually Kage's are one of the strongest, if not the strongest, ninja in his or her respective village. Kages are responsible for making all the important decisions for the village and also responsible for the well being of all of the village's inhabitants. Kage's are handpicked by the previous Kage of the village.

Chakra

What Is Chakra?

Chakra is best described as the special **inner energy** a ninja needs to perform certain techniques. It is one of the most important elements in fighting for a ninja. There are **2** main parts to Chakra, **body energy and spiritual energy**. Body energy comes from the **cells** in your body. How much energy you have depends on how fast you can move the cells in your body. Body energy is important because it provides strength for a ninja's mind. Spiritual energy comes from the **experience** of a ninja. The more experience a ninja has the more spiritual energy he or she will have. Spiritual energy can be best described as an adrenaline rush or just an extra burst of energy that comes into use when a ninja is very tired or worn out.

Controlling chakra is very important in battle. In order to perform certain techniques, ninjas have to build up a certain amount of chakra. Genjutsu and Ninjutsu techniques need chakra to be performed correctly. Chakra is created from the **stamina** of a ninja.

A ninja must have a certain amount of chakra in their body to live.

Inside a ninja there is a special circulatory system that transfers chakra throughout the body. There are certain pipes and passage ways that transfer the chakra. There are 361 openings in the chakra circulatory system that wind all around the important organs in a person's body. Each chakra opening is called **Tenketsu**. When all of the Tenketsus are blocked inside a ninja's body, the ninja will be unable to perform any techniques.

In addition to openings for chakra, there are also gates that limit the flow of chakra. There are a total of **8 gates** inside a ninja's body. Controlling the amount of chakra flowing is very important because it prevents a ninja from using too much chakra and possibly cause serious damage.

POJO'S UNOFFICIAL TOTAL NARUTO!
This book is not sponsored, endorsed by, or otherwise affiliated with any of the companies or products featured in this book.
This is not an official publication.

When all 8 gates are opened, there are no limits to the amount of chakra and the ninja is at full strength. However, opening all 8 gates can be fatal depending on the technique the ninja is performing.

There are **5** different types of Chakra: **Earth, Fire, Lightning, Water, and Wind.**

Most of the time, the type of chakra you have depends on genetics and where you are from. People of the Uchiha clan usually have Fire chakra. Most Jonin can use at least **2** types of chakra. In order to find out what kind of chakra a ninja has, the ninja uses a piece of paper from a tree that feeds off chakra. If the paper splits, then the type of chakra you have is wind. If it bursts into flames, the type of chakra is fire. If it gets soggy, then the chakra is of the water type. If the paper crumples, then it is lightning. And finally, if the paper turns into dust, then the type of chakra is Earth.

POJO'S UNOFFICIAL TOTAL NARUTO!
This book is not sponsored, endorsed by, or otherwise affiliated with any of the companies or products featured in this book.
This is not an official publication.

Bloodlines

Inheritance

Bloodline limits are special **inherited** traits or techniques passed down from generation to generation. Most of the time, these traits are passed down within a clan. Bloodline limits can increase the strength, speed, or endurance of a ninja which gives the ninja a special advantage in combat.

Byakugan

The Bykugan is a special bloodline of the **Hyuga** clan. This bloodline is a special ability in the **eye**. The Byakugan allows the user to see all the critical areas inside of a ninja such as where the chakra is stored. Sometimes a very advanced Byakugan user can also neutralize the

Tenketsu and stop chakra flow, eventually killing the opposition. Another special power of the Byakugan is the ability for the user to see in 360 degrees or **panoramic** view.

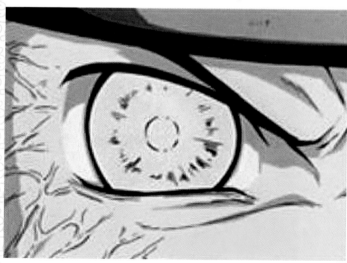

Hyoton

This is a special bloodline trait that Haku has. All of the previous users have died off and Haku was the last user. This bloodline is believed to have originated in the Village Hidden in the Mist. This bloodline gives the user a special ability to manipulate **ice** with **2** techniques. One technique gives the user the ability to place ice mirrors all around the opponent which confuses the opponent. Then the user can travel from mirror to mirror to attack the opponent with the other special technique, which are deadly flying ice needles.

POJO'S UNOFFICIAL TOTAL NARUTO!
This book is not sponsored, endorsed by, or otherwise affiliated with any of the companies or products featured in this book.
This is not an official publication.

Dead Bone Pulse

This is a special bloodline trait of the people from the Kaguya clan. Kimimaro is the only member left in the clan, so he is the only person seen using this bloodline. This special ability allows Kiminaro to alter his bone structure. He can manipulate his bones to poke out spikes out of his normal body structure. These bones are very solid, like steel.

Sharingan

This is the signature bloodline limit of the Uchiha clan. There is only 1 person who has this special trait and is not from the Uchiha clan, Kakashi. He received the Sharingan from a member of the Uchiha Clan and it was surgically implanted into his eye socket. The Sharingan gives the user the ability to copy and see through all types of techniques. The use of the Sharingan can be seen by the **color of the eye** of the person, which becomes red with small black markings

POJO'S UNOFFICIAL TOTAL NARUTO!
This book is not sponsored, endorsed by, or otherwise affiliated with any of the companies or products featured in this book.
This is not an official publication.

41

Attack Types

Main Categories

Genjutsu

Genjutsu techniques are generally illusionary techniques that cause the opponent to **hallucinate** and see things that really do not exist. Genjutsu techniques are useful to confuse the opponent.

Taijutsu

Taijutsu is **hand-to-hand** combat. There is no chakra or hand seals involved. Standard punching and kicking is considered Taijutsu. Rock Lee is the only ninja that specializes solely with Taijutsu.

Ninjutsu

Ninjutsu is the art of performing **hand seals** and using chakra to perform the techniques. Performing Ninjutsu is probably the most difficult because it requires a lot of concentration to execute the hand seal. Ninjutsu techniques usually take just a few seconds to execute and are probably the most commonly used type of technique.

Detailed/Special Categories

Dojutsu

These techniques are performed with the eye. These include the Sharingan and Byakugan. Dojutsu techniques are usually performed by those who come from a clan with a special bloodline limit or those with extreme skill.

Hijutsu

These techniques are ones that can only be performed by a specific ninja or by those specific of a clan. Usually the hijutsu technique is the strongest technique that a ninja possess. An example of Hijutsu is Haku's Ice Mirrors. (Page 76).

Kinjutsu

These techniques are ones that are banned by the Kages. It is illegal to perform them. Kinjutsu techniques are ones that can cause major damage when used. An example of a kinjutsu that is sinister in its nature is **Orochimaru's Edo Tensei.**

POJO'S UNOFFICIAL TOTAL NARUTO!
This book is not sponsored, endorsed by, or otherwise affiliated with any of the companies or products featured in this book.
This is not an official publication.

43

the MAJOR STORY ARCS

By: Nick Meisner

The Disaster of the Nine-Tailed Fox and the Start of Squad 7!

Thirteen years ago, a mysterious fox suddenly appeared in The Village Hidden in the Leaves. Fortunately for the Leaf Village, they had a hero named **"The Fourth Hokage"** who was able to defeat the destructive beast and seal it in a newborn baby at the cost of his own life. The baby himself grew up to be Naruto Uzumaki, the number-one hyperactive knucklehead ninja of the Leaf Village, and the container of the **Nine-Tailed Fox**. Because of the demon sealed inside him, Naruto is shunned for most of his childhood until he begins meeting people who care for him. After failing three times to become a ninja, Naruto finally passes the exam to become a **Genin** (starting level ninja) with some help from his teacher, Iruka Umino. Shortly after, Naruto is assigned to his team consisting of two other Genin, Sakura Haruno and Sasuke Uchiha, and their **Jonin** (high level ninja) team leader, Kakashi Hatake. Despite Sakura's infatuation with Sasuke and her disgust with Naruto, the three of them become friends after a tough trial of stealing bells from their teacher. Once they figure out that teamwork was the key to being a ninja, Kakashi grants the three of them full ninja status, and the title of **Squad 7!**

The Mysterious Rogue Ninja, Zabuza and the Great Naruto Bridge!

With a few simple missions under their belt, Naruto begs The Hokage to give them a mission that is more difficult. He assigns them the task of guarding Tazuna, a bridge builder from the Land of Waves, as they escort him back to his homeland. Tazuna is being hunted by a Rogue Ninja, Zabuza, who has been hired to kill him. Upon entering the Land of Waves, they encounter Zabuza. Kakashi seems to defeat him using his **Sharingan Eye**. Zabuza's body is carried away by another mysterious ninja posing as an **Anbu** from the Mist Village. The team learns that Tazuna is trying to complete a bridge to the mainland to help his poor nation. Gato, who doesn't like this idea, hired Zabuza to kill Tazuna. While the bridge is nearing completion, Zabuza attacks again, this time with the mysterious Mist Village ninja, Haku,

as his partner. A major battle ensues with Naruto and Sasuke fighting Haku, leaving Kakashi to fight against Zabuza. Sasuke activates his bloodline trait, the **Sharingan**, for the first time in a desperate attempt to beat Haku's ice style jutsu. Sasuke is beaten to the point of near death, and upon seeing this; Naruto activates the power of the Nine-Tailed Fox to save Sasuke and beat Haku. Meanwhile, Kakashi uses his most powerful jutsu, the **Lightning Blade**, to finish off Zabuza. Haku sees this, and jumps in front of Kakashi's electrified arm, dying to save Zabuza. Upon seeing the death of his friend and partner, Zabuza turns on Gato, killing him. Zabuza and Haku both die together on the bridge that they tried to stop from being built. In honor of the great courage Naruto showed by fighting Haku and saving the village, the Land of Waves names their bridge "The Great Naruto Bridge!"

Survival in the Forest of Death, and the Chunin Preliminaries!

Six months after the mission in the Land of Waves, the Chunin exams are beginning, giving each village's Genin ninja a chance to get promoted. Ninja from all over come to the Hidden Leaf Village to participate in the examination. Among them are three ninja from the Hidden Sand Village, Gaara, Temari, and Kankuro. After making a rather rude impression, all of the ninja proceed to the exam halls in the academy. The finishing teams are taken to **The Forest of Death** to have an all out survival match, with the goal being to reach the center of the forest for the third part of the exam. Team 7 has a rather unfortunate encounter with a Grass Village ninja using the **power of snakes**; he beats Sasuke and Naruto to near death. In the fight, the ninja seals Naruto off from his Nine-Tailed Fox abilities, and leaves a mysterious curse mark on Sasuke's neck. Shortly thereafter the Sound Village Ninja attack them in their state of weakness. Sasuke awakens the new curse mark, giving him power to rival a Hokage. He makes quick work of the ninja, but at the cost of severe damage to his body. The team eventually makes it to the third exam area, where a tournament is announced. The top winners will proceed to the final rounds of the Chunin Exam. Sasuke defeats Yoroi, Naruto beats Kiba, Shino beats Zaku, Neji defeats his cousin Hinata, Temari quickly shuts down Tenten, Kankuro easily defeats Murusame, Dosu makes quick work of Choji, and Gaara struggles to beat Lee; only succeeding after crushing both Lee's left arm and leg in sand. With that, the winners are told that the finals will be held in one month. All the Genin leave to take a good long break for training.

POJO'S UNOFFICIAL TOTAL NARUTO!

Naruto and Sasuke's Dangerous New Training!

After the tournament, Kakashi decides to take Sasuke under his wing for training. Being as Sasuke is similar in fighting style to Kakashi, he figures it would be the best thing he could do for Sasuke. Unfortunately, this leaves poor Naruto alone to train with Ebisu, a Special Jonin trainer, who's not a very good teacher. They head to train at the Leaf Village Hot Springs, where they encounter a mysterious man on a toad. He is known as the Toad Sage, Jiraiya. After Naruto sees Jiraiya defeat Ebisu with ease, he begs Jiraiya to be his new teacher. Naruto eventually persuades Jiraiya to become his trainer.

Jiraiya figures Naruto would be best at summoning toads like he can, and after removing Naruto's seal from the Grass Ninja, he leaves him to it. Three weeks pass with little progress, until Jiraiya puts Naruto in a life or death situation. With the Fox's help Naruto summons **Gamabunta**, the boss of the toad world, to save him. Armed with a new jutsu, Naruto heads to the Chunin finals.

A Secret Plot?! The Destruction of the Hidden Leaf Village!

*In the center of the Leaf Village, the final tournament starts. Sasuke and Gaara are supposed to have their match first, but unfortunately, Sasuke is nowhere to be found. The Third Hokage postpones the match, and allows Naruto to fight Neji. Fighting to prove his worth, and to avenge Hinata for what Neji did to her, Naruto is able to defeat Neji. With the crowd in cheers, Naruto heads back to the waiting area to give his buddy Shikamaru the best of luck in his match. Shikamaru takes on Temari using his shadows to attempt to capture her. The fight between the two of them is a true battle of wits, and in the end, Shikamaru proves victorious by capturing her in his **Shadow Possession Jutsu**. However, he has run out of chakra, and surrenders the match, giving Temari a free win. Shino and Kankuro are the next in line. Kankuro, afraid that their plan for the Leaf Village might be foiled if he shows his new jutsu, surrenders the match without lifting a finger. Sasuke and Gaara are the only ones left to fight, and there is no sign of Sasuke. Gaara takes the field and waits for his opponent. Finally, in a shower of leaves, Sasuke appears, ready to fight. As the battle starts, Gaara shields himself in a sand coccon and begins chanting, as if getting ready for some major transformation. Sasuke fears*

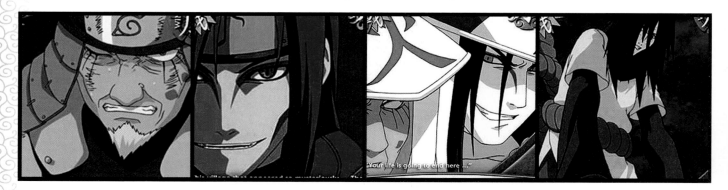

that only bad could come from that, so he activates his dangerous new jutsu, **Chidori!** Instantly, the crowd recognizes it as Kakashi's Lightning Blade jutsu, and cheers. Sasuke charges at Gaara, piercing his cocoon and hitting him in the shoulder. Gaara runs from the stadium as an explosion is heard, and the crowd is put to sleep with a jutsu. The Third Hokage now has a **kunai knife** to his throat, held there by the mysterious grass ninja, Orochimaru. He reveals that he is from the Sound Village, and he has plotted with the Sand to destroy the Leaf. The

Third Hokage escapes from his grasp, and heads to the roof of the building for a battle with Orochimaru. Meanwhile, Naruto, Sakura, and Sasuke are sent to chase after Gaara. Back on the rooftops, The Third Hokage is in a deadlock with Orochimaru. He runs to Orochimaru, grabbing his arms, and gets a sword run through his chest. With his strength fading, The Third Hokage summons the ultimate jutsu, the **Reaper Death Seal**. Using the same jutsu that The Fourth Hokage used on the Fox, he seals Orochimaru's arms inside himself, and dies in

the process. Without arms to make hand signs, jutsu will never be able to be used by Orochimaru again. The Third Hokage saves the village, but at the cost of his own life. In the forest, Team 7 is fighting Gaara with little luck. Gaara is also a demon container like Naruto, and has become possessed by the One-Tailed Beast, Shukaku. Using his new summoning Jutsu, Naruto calls out Gamabunta to take on Shukaku. Naruto and Gamabunta emerge victorious from the fight, but Team 7 is devastated to learn that The Third Hokage had died.

The Recovery of the Leaf Village, and the Search for Tsunade!

With the repairs to the Leaf Village underway, the elders on the council see the need for a Fifth Hokage. They call for Jiraiya, one of the **Sannin**, to lead the village. As a bookwriter and "researcher" he is none to fond of the idea. However, his teammate Tsunade would be the perfect fit, and he takes Naruto to search with him, promising to teach Naruto a jutsu more powerful than even Chidori. Jiraiya and Naruto catch up with her in a gambling town not far from the Leaf Village. Along the way, Jiraiya has been training Naruto to whirl Chakra in his palm for an attack type jutsu. Jiraiya is surprised when he sees Orochimaru trying to make a deal with Tsunade to heal his arms. All three Sannin are finally reunited, and it only leads to a three-cornered deadlock. With Orochimaru unable to use any major jutsu, he

is quickly defeated. In an act of bravery, Naruto uses his new **swirling chakra** jutsu, Rasengan, to beat Kabuto and save Tsunade from his attacks. Tsunade agrees to be the Hokage, and proceeds with the two of them back to the Leaf Village.

Sasuke, a Rogue Ninja?! The Uchiha's Thirst for Power!

Upon arriving back in the village, Naruto decides to visit Sasuke, who had been severely injured in his fight with Gaara. Sasuke has seen Naruto's power in the fight with Gaara, and is furious that Naruto has surpassed him, and took out the demon that he couldn't. He challenges Naruto to a duel on the roof of the hospital. In the heated battle, both Naruto and Sasuke use their **ultimate jutsu** to try to defeat the other. Not wanting his students to kill each other, Kakashi jumps in and stops the fight. Sasuke feels that he has won, until he realizes how much more damage Rasengan did to the surrounding area. Orochimaru, still in search of a way to heal his arms, sends four of his **Sound Ninja** to persuade Sasuke to join them. The Sound Ninja offer to teach Sasuke the true power of the curse mark. The Sound Four prepare for the journey by giving Sasuke power enhancing pills, and putting him in a barrel to rest.

With the promise of power at hand, Sasuke leaves the village with the Sound Four.

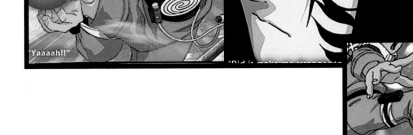

POJO'S UNOFFICIAL TOTAL NARUTO!
This book is not sponsored, endorsed by, or otherwise affiliated with any of the companies or products featured in this book.
This is not an official publication.

51

A Final Confrontation!
The Battle at the Valley of the End!

With most of the Chunin and Jonin out on missions, Tsunade is left to form a team to chase Sasuke by using the last Chunin available, Shikamaru. As the only one to get promoted, he requests Naruto, Choji, Neji, and Kiba to help on the mission.

They first run into Jirobo, a ninja who **eats chakra**. Choji handles the battle, and is able to defeat and kill Jirobo, at the cost of severe damage to his own body. Kidomaru is a master of ranged combat, and Neji is able to defeat him, but not after getting shot by one of Kidomaru's arrows. Sakon is a ninja who is a **living parasite**, and attacks Kiba. The team moves on to encounter Tayuya, a **genjutsu flute master**; Shikamaru decides to take her.

At this point, a fifth sound ninja, Kimmimaro, joins the battle and takes the barrel containing Sasuke. Shikamaru urges Naruto to chase him, and the team becomes fully separated. Naruto tries his best to defeat Kimmimaro, but fails. Rock Lee has been trailing the team, determined to prove his abilities fresh after his surgery. In the nick of time, Lee jumps in to save Naruto.

Out from the barrel comes Sasuke, laughing, running off towards the Sound Village. Naruto leaves Lee to handle Kimmimaro and he heads towards Sasuke. Kiba, Shikamaru, and Lee are having trouble taking down their opponents in their curse mark powered states; until help arrives.

The Sand gennin have returned to help the Leaf ninja, and with the added help, Kankuro is able to trap Sakon, Temari blows Tayuya away with her wind , and Gaara sends Kimmimaro underground with his Sand Tomb jutsu. Unfortunately for Naruto, Sasuke refuses to return to the Leaf Village. Naruto knows the only way to bring Sasuke back is to beat him unconscious. The

'Oh... I'm a bit loopy.'   'Chidori!'   Whenever he gets stuck on a move, he does tl

POJO'S UNOFFICIAL TOTAL NARUTO!
This book is not sponsored, endorsed by, or otherwise affiliated with any of the companies or products featured in this book.
This is not an official publication.

heated fight presses on until both are left exhausted. Sasuke has gone into his **state two** curse mark form, giving him wings. Naruto has transformed into his feral state using the Fox's power. Sasuke is determined to break his bonds with the Leaf Village, and Naruto is determined

to save them. With nothing left to say, they charge at each other, launching their ultimate jutsu, Rasengan and Chidori. They collide, and in the aftermath, Sasuke is left standing above an unconscious Naruto. He drops his Leaf headband, and heads off to Orochimaru. Kakashi

carries a severely wounded Naruto back to the village to recover.

While in the hospital, Naruto is visited by Jiraiya, who offers to personally train him for three years away from the village. With newfound hope of rescuing Sasuke, Naruto accepts.

VIDEO GAME REVIEWS

Ratings System
Poor ✿ Fair ✿✿
Good ✿✿✿ Very Good ✿✿✿✿
Excellent ✿✿✿✿✿

Naruto: Ultimate Ninja
by Namco

Aug 8, 2006 · Playstation2

Over 12 playable characters.

The Characters looks more like manga drawings than anime cells.

Graphics have a feel like SupersmashBrothers.

A pretty good fighter and now under $20 due to its age.

Pojo's Review: ✿✿✿✿

Naruto Ultimate Ninja 2

by Namco

Jun 12, 2007 · Playstation2

Over 30 playable characters.

Earn points towards upgrading a character's strength, defense, chakra, agility, and even special abilities.

Beautiful cut scenes. Good voice-overs. Great gameplay!

Pojo's Rating: ⦿⦿⦿⦿ 1/2

Naruto: Ultimate Ninja 3

By Namco

Mar 25, 2008 · Playstation2

Choose from over 40 characters.

This game offers English and Japanese voice-overs.

Over 55 missions in Ultimate Contest mode

Turn some of your favorite characters into more powerful ninja warriors and summon giant creatures as allies.

Pojo's Rating: ⦿⦿⦿⦿

Naruto: Uzumaki Chronicles

by Namco

Nov 16, 2006 · Playstation2

Visuals are great, but the game play is poor. Not much of a storyline in this one … just pointless missions. Battles are repetitive.

Pojo's Rating: ⦿⦿

POJO'S UNOFFICIAL TOTAL NARUTO!
This book is not sponsored, endorsed by, or otherwise affiliated with any of the companies or products featured in this book.
This is not an official publication.

55

Naruto Uzumaki Chronicles 2
by Namco

Sep 4, 2007 · Playstation2

*A slight improvement over Naruto Uzumaki Chronicles 1.
Original Storyline.*

You can play cooperatively with a friend, an enjoyable aspect.

Pojo's Rating: 🌀🌀🌀 1/2

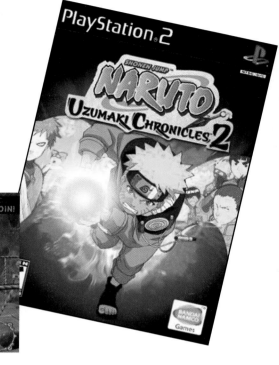

Naruto Ultimate Ninja Heroes
by Namco

Release Date: Aug 28, 2007 · Sony PSP

20 playable characters. Wi-Fi enabled. Not much of a storyline. Just arcade type fighting. Long Load times.

Pojo's Rating: 🌀🌀🌀

Naruto: Ultimate Ninja Heroes 2: The Phantom Fortress
by Namco

Release Date: Jun 24, 2008 · Sony PSP

Over 20 playable characters. This game offers a better storyline than the original. Pretty simple learning curve, good gameplay, and good graphics.

Pojo's Rating: ◎◎◎ 1/2

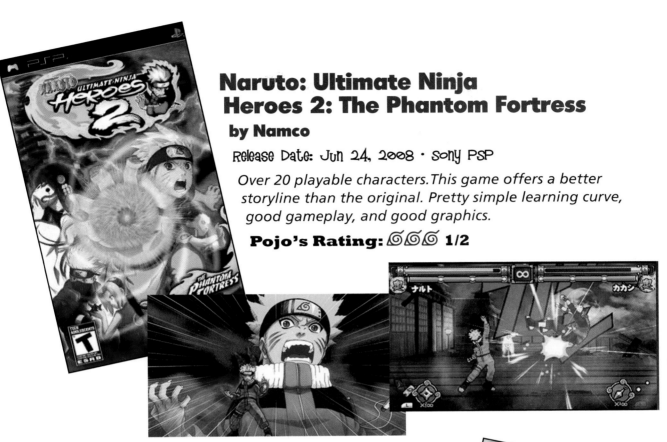

Naruto: Rise of a Ninja
by UBI Soft

October 30, 2007 · Xbox 360

Basically a playable version of Season 1 of the anime.

Great graphics and great Leaf Village details.

More of an adventure game than a fighting game.

Pojo's Rating: ◎◎◎◎◎

POJO'S UNOFFICIAL TOTAL NARUTO!
This book is not sponsored, endorsed by, or otherwise affiliated with any of the companies or products featured in this book.
This is not an official publication.

57

Naruto: Ninja Destiny

by Tomy

February 27, 2008 · Nintendo DS

16 characters from the anime.

Game modes include storyline, multiplayer, and versus.

Graphics are pretty good for the DS, but the fighting isn't all that great.

Pojo's Rating: 🌀🌀🌀

Naruto: Ninja Council

by Tomy

Mar 7, 2006 · Game Boy Advance

This is a side scrolling type action game.

Play as Naruto, Sasuke, and Kakashi.

Graphics aren't all that great. Music is bad. Game play is average.

Pojo's Rating: 🌀🌀 1/2

Naruto Ninja Council 2

by Tomy

Oct 4, 2006 · Game Boy Advance

An improvement over Ninja Council 1.

Switch between Naruto, Sasuke and Sakura characters on the fly.

The game loosely follows Seasons 2 & 3 of the anime.

Game play is pretty challenging.

Pojo's rating: 🌀🌀🌀 1/2

Naruto: Ninja Council 3

by Tomy

May 22, 2007 · Nintendo DS

Similar game play to Ninja Council 1 & 2.

Over 25 playable characters from the show.

No storyline, Just missions.

Easily beaten in just a few hours, and gets old quick.

Pojo's Rating: 🌀🌀🌀

POJO'S UNOFFICIAL TOTAL NARUTO!
This book is not sponsored, endorsed by, or otherwise affiliated with any of the companies or products featured in this book.
This is not an official publication.

59

Naruto: Path of The Ninja

by Tomy

October 23, 2007 · Nintendo DS

Six playable characters from the show.

This is a Role Playing Adventure Game (not a straight fighting game like the others).

Some parts, like many RPG's, get repetitive.

Graphics are not great for a DS game, but good game play for Naruto fans.

Pojo's Rating: ⊘⊘⊘ 1/2

Naruto Clash of Ninja

by Tomy

February 9, 2006 · GameCube

The first Naruto fighting game for the Gamecube.

Ten playable characters.

Graphics are great.

One of the best Fighting games for the Gamecube (besides Super Smash Brothers).

Pojo's Rating: ⊘⊘⊘⊘

POJO'S UNOFFICIAL TOTAL NARUTO!

Naruto Clash of Ninja 2
by D3 Publisher

September 11, 2006 · GameCube

23 playable characters.

Great Graphics and a good fighting engine

If you still play your Gamecube, and are looking for a fighter, this game is worth picking up.

Pojo's Rating: 🌀🌀🌀🌀

Naruto: Clash of Ninja Revolution
by D3 Publisher

October 23, 2007 · Nintendo Wii

Over 15 playable characters.

Story mode is not satisfying.

Game feels a bit awkward and clumsy with the Wii Remotes.

The game plays much better with GameCube controllers.

Pojo's Rating: 🌀🌀🌀 1/2

POJO'S UNOFFICIAL TOTAL NARUTO!
This book is not sponsored, endorsed by, or otherwise affiliated with any of the companies or products featured in this book.
This is not an official publication.

61

DECK BUILDING TIPS

By: Eduardo "Beastly Mage" Miller

Here are some tips to build your Naruto CCG deck.

#1: Watch your cards:

First, some numbers for you:

- *A deck has to have 40 cards. No more. No less.*
- *No more than 25 and no less than one should be single-named Ninjas (example: Ninjas such as **Naruto Uzumaki, ([Pure Anger] n-256))**.*

POJO'S UNOFFICIAL TOTAL NARUTO!
This book is not sponsored, endorsed by, or otherwise affiliated with any of the companies or products featured in this book.
This is not an official publication.

The rest of the cards could be:

- Platoon Ninjas (Ninjas with more than one name, such as **Naruto Uzumaki & Gamakichi** ([Son's Favor], n-us079)).
- Missions (such as **Bingo Book** (m-011))
- Clients (such as **Inari** (c-001))
- Jutsus (such as **Wind Style: Great Breakthrough** (j-079)).

#2: Balance your elements:

What sort of **elements** (symbols) are you thinking of using? Maybe Fire? Or perhaps Earth? Remember that to pay for hand costs (for Missions and Ninjas), and Jutsu costs you need to meet certain requirements, particularly with the element symbols. A good idea is to have no **more than two** main elements in your deck, but a single-element deck works even better. Of course, it all depends on your strategy. That doesn't mean that cards that have other elements can't be used (for example: in a Fire-Water deck you can use such cards as **Sakura Haruno** ([A Double Personality], n-us006) and **Shikamaru Nara** ([Formation], n-us014).

POJO'S UNOFFICIAL TOTAL NARUTO!
This book is not sponsored, endorsed by, or otherwise affiliated with any of the companies or products featured in this book.
This is not an official publication.

63

#3: Cover all bases:

In order to have a good deck, you must see to it that you have enough **Ninjas** to cover all turns possible, from turn 0 and so on. A certain amount of Ninjas for every turn you're thinking of covering is a good idea.

#4: To side deck or not to side deck:

A side deck **can't** have more or less than **10** cards. You can repeat names of cards found in your main deck, but **can't** have more than **three** cards with the same name in your deck and side deck combined. For example: you can have two Shikamaru cards in your deck, and one in your side deck, but not more than that. Note: a side deck is not mandatory.

#5: Rare does not always mean good:

*When building a deck, remember that a card's true worth is not determined by how rare or how shiny it is (or even how expensive), but how good it is for **your strategy**.*

#6: Themes:

*Sometimes, a deck with a theme works great. A deck centered on a certain character (or characters) can be good. For example: **Hyuga Clan** decks, **Sharingan** decks (with characters such as **Kakashi, Sasuke,** and **Itachi**), etc.*

#7:
Have fun!

Need we say more?!

Notes:

- *You should have no more than three Ninja cards with the same name (for example: you can have three **"Gaara of the Desert"** ([Conversation] n-145) cards, three **"Gaara of the Desert (Possessed Mode)"** ([Possessed Mode], n-179), and three **"Shukaku"** ([Perfect Posession], n-177) cards in a deck). While these cards count as one **"Gaara of the Desert"** card in your village or in the battlefield, they don't count towards the three-card limit when in your deck, since the primary name (the one in big letters) is the one that counts towards the card limit. The secondary name (the one found with the characteristics) only counts while the card is in play.*

- *Platoon cards, even if you have three of one of the necessary Ninjas in your deck, don't count as the same Ninja. For example, you can have three **Naruto Uzumaki** cards, three **Gamakichi** cards, and three **Naruto Uzumaki** and **Gamakichi** cards in your deck.*
- *The three-card limit also counts for Jutsu, Mission, and Client cards.*
- *Some Client cards have two names. The same rule that applies to Ninja cards applies to Client cards too.*
- *Even if the cards have the same name, they don't need to have the same effect.*

POJO'S UNOFFICIAL TOTAL NARUTO!
This book is not sponsored, endorsed by, or otherwise affiliated with any of the companies or products featured in this book.
This is not an official publication.

65

The CRAZY ANIMAL MILL!

By: Mark Howard

This is a crazy **fast** Mill deck! The goal of this deck is to get the animals out and use mill cards and Jutsu to **cut cards off your opponent's deck** until there's nothing left, and they lose by default. Cards like **One Morning, Reunion,** and other **draw** cards practically give this Deck an automatic win! Your opponent will think twice about draw power.

Use cards like **Kiba MBC** to get **Akamaru** for milling, and to get the **Wolf** out faster. **Tsume** also teams up with it well. And cards like **Dynamic Marking** and **Wolf Fang Over Fang** can smack tons of cards off, especially if you use **All Fours Jutsu** beforehand!

Sakura, Ino, and the **Hokage,** among other things, are great for stalling and letting the opponent's deck shrink. In fact, this Sakura is just the most splashable and durable stall card in the game!

Among the ways to thin out your Deck, **Just Like Drifting Clouds** lets you recycle your hand and get a fresh one, and you even get a free card for doing that! This way, you can

"if I were you, I'd let Akamaru go."

Kiba Inuzuka

Leaf | Genin | Male | Growth

[MAN BEAST CLONE]
When this Ninja is put in play, you can search for 1 "Akamaru" Ninja card in your Deck, show it to your opponent and place it in your hand. Then, shuffle your Deck.

2/0

"Kuromaru, let's go!"

Tsume Inuzuka

Leaf | Jonin | Female

[COMBINATION]
Valid: When this Ninja is sent out to Battle with an "Animal" Ninja in the same Team, it gets +1/+1 during the turn.

5/1

Crazy Animal Mill Deck

Ninjas - 25

Turn 0
2x Kiba Inuzuka [Man Beast Clone]
Sasuke Uchiha [Rivalry]
3x Sakura Haruno [Toughness] (The Chosen Starter Deck)
Ino Yamanaka [Formation]

Turn 1
3x Akamaru [Ninja Art of Beast Mimicry]
2x Sasuke Uchiha [Firm Determination] (Shonen Jump promo)
Shikamaru [Formation]
Kiba Inuzuka [Bond with Akamaru]

Turn 2
None

Turn 3
Hayate Gekko [Judgment]
2x Double Headed Wolf [Risky New Jutsu]

Turn 4
3x Tsume Inuzuka [Combination]
2x Kuromaru [Partner]

Turn 5
Kakashi Hatake [Team Leader]
Kakashi Hatake [Gifted Ninja of the Leaf Village]

Turn 6
The Third Hokage [Addressing Past Wrongs] or [Professor]

Missions - 4

2x Just Like Drifting Clouds
Man-Beast Transformation Combo
Another Way

Jutsu - 11

2x Fang Over Fang
3x Ninja Art of Beast Mimicry: All Fours Jutsu
2x 8 Trigram Divination Seal Spell Formula
Chidori (Quest for Power Starter Deck version)
2x Wolf Fang Over Fang
Dynamic Marking

cycle your Deck and pick out staples like **Kiba, Wolf,** and **Dynamic Marking**. Watch your opponent wish they could use draw power!

One of the most important tactics for this Deck is stalling. You will rarely ever want to attack your opponent. Wait and block, then use All four Jutsus on your Wolf and following up with Wolf Fang Over Fang to smack them for a win, chomp a quarter of their full Deck away, AND scare them out of attacking you again! If you can beat them with a one-**Chakra Jutsu**, they won't be crazy enough for another round. **Clouds** will constantly recycle your hand. There's no way to predict if you have All Fours!

Kiba Inuzuka

Leaf | Genin | Male | Animal | Growth

[BOND WITH AKAMARU]
When this Ninja is put in play, you can put 1 "Akamaru" Ninja card in your Discard Pile or your Chakra area in play.

2/0

Note:

A Mill Deck tries to win by making your opponent burn through his cards very quickly. If your opponent can't draw a card, you win!

POJO'S UNOFFICIAL TOTAL NARUTO!
This book is not sponsored, endorsed by, or otherwise affiliated with any of the companies or products featured in this book.
This is not an official publication.

67

Earth/Lightning Deck

This Deck is all about Control!

By: Mark Howard

It's important to have more Ninjas than the opponent, and you'll have lots of leftover Ninjas to chump block with. This deck can also block **Mental Decks** to a standpoint, and stall them out. It doesn't end there, because you'll be able to use Mental Battles through Sakura, who will be an unstoppable defense early in, and First Chunin Exam.

This Deck has **combos** crawling all over the place. Just look at the deck list and watch all the combos pop up, like **Iruka and Naruto [Pure Anger]**, and the legendary Gaara-Shika-Cho combo! Gama and Sakura stall it out until crucial cards, like **Jiraiya and Naruto** to recycle Jutsu, the Hokage, Guy, and the Shik/Asuma platoon pop up. Use your **Jutsu** and **Mission** cards to stall and draw things. Disable your opponent's cards with **Ino, Sexy Jutsu, Rasengan, Chunin Exam, and Caged Bird,** and then go in for the kill.

Basically, you want to dominate in the amount of Ninjas you have, and stall until a deck runs out, or you get your good cards. Ino will do wonders for you there while **Neji, Gaara, and Dosu** are good to kamikaze with late-game.

This deck's best combo (which is nearly everyone's) is **Gaara-Shika-Cho. Shikamaru.** This lets **Choji** hit the opponent, and then Gaara launches Choji to kill them.

This is a flexible deck, but you'll need to practice with it. The cards in it also aren't too expensive, so it's a great affordable deck that can change its play style to counter many different decks!

Earth/Lightning Deck

Ninjas – 25

Turn 0
2x Ino Yamanaka [Formation]
2x Choji Akimichi [Formation]
Naruto Uzumaki [Mastering a Secret Technique]
Naruto Uzumaki [Rivalry]
Sasuke Uchiha [Rivalry]

Turn 1
2x Shikamaru Nara [Formation]
2x Sakura Haruno [Teamwork Between High IQ Ninjas]
Dosu Kinuta [Targeted Prey]

Turn 2
2x Iruka Umino [Accurate Analysis]
Gama [Heteromorphy]
Naruto Uzumaki [Pure Anger]
Neji Hyuga [For Those Who Believe in Me]
Gaara of the Desert [Tragic Name]

Turn 3
None

Turn 4
2x Asuma Sarutobi [Barbecue]

Turn 5
2x Might Guy [Countermeasure Against the Sharingan Eye]/[Backup]

Turn 6
2x Jiraiya [Instruction of the Hidden Technique
The First Hokage [The One who Created the Village]
(Quest for Power Starter Deck)

Missions – 7
After the Battle
2x Reunion with the Former Teacher
2x Caged Bird
2x First Chunin Exam

Jutsu - 7
Kunai [Eternal Rivalry]
2x Thinking Mode
2x Rasengan (Quest for Power Starter Deck)
2x S. Jutsu (Curse of the Sand) J-110

Platoons – 1
Shikamaru Nara & Asuma Sarutobi [Shogi Match]

POJO'S UNOFFICIAL TOTAL NARUTO!
This book is not sponsored, endorsed by, or otherwise affiliated with any of the companies or products featured in this book.
This is not an official publication.

69

FREEDORI DECK

Free use of a Jutsu card...
Who doesn't love that
in this game?

By: Eduardo "Beastly Mage" Miller

The center of the Freedori (as in Free Chidori) deck is simple;
use one of the most feared Jutsus in the game without
paying the cost.

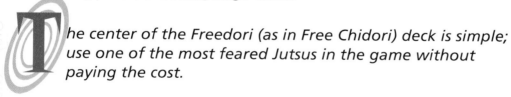

1-Sasuke Uchiha [Beyond the Limits] (n-155)

This Ninja's effect is simple: "This Ninja can use the 'Chidori' Jutsu card without paying the
Jutsu cost." For the Freedori deck, at least two copies of this card in the deck is a good idea.

2-Chidori:

There are several versions of this Jutsu card out there. The best (and rarest) one is j-131, from
Revenge and Rebirth, giving +5/+0 and one extra damage to every Ninja battling the user (either
Kakashi or Sasuke) when the user scores a Victory or Outstanding Victory.

3-Kakashi Hatake:

Now, what's a deck centered on a technique without the guy who actually created it? There
are three versions you should consider:

[The Past in 10 Years Ago] (n-185): Giving growth to your Kakashis is good. Take into
consideration that when you put in play a Ninja with a Hand Cost by means of Growth you don't

POJO'S UNOFFICIAL TOTAL NARUTO!
This book is not sponsored, endorsed by, or otherwise affiliated with any of the companies or products featured in this book.
This is not an official publication.

have to pay the hand cost AND you still get the Chakra you need.

[Early Settlement] (n-064): This is, by far, the best Kakashi ever. Being able to get a Battle Reward by means of a Victory or Outstanding Victory brings you closer to winning the game.

[The Worst Outcome] (n-293): You can move to your hand a Genin-Level Ninja from your discard pile at the end of the turn he was sent out to battle. This can allow you to recover such Ninjas as Sasuke (n-155) and others.

4-Sharingan Eye (j-007):

Since the main Ninjas in this deck are both Sharingan users, this simple negation Jutsu fits quite well here.

Now, there's other cards to consider, such as 8 Triagram Divination Seal Spell Formula (j-006), which provides a certain level of negation (by means of field removal). Another card to consider is Just Like Drifting Clouds (m-us086), bringing draw power and deck cycling to the Freedori deck. Also, Tide of the Deadly Combat (m-092) can turn the tables on your opponent. One last mission to consider is A Shadow In the Moonlight (m-us077). This mission is Fire's equivalent to Bingo Book (m-011), and can help move important Ninjas to your hand.

Now, not all cards in this deck should be Fire. Lightning cards such as Naruto Uzumaki [Legacy of the Fourth Hokage] (n-187), Shikamaru Nara [Formation] (n-us014), and Sakura Haruno [A Double Personality] (n-us006) are good cards for this deck. But, the best idea for a Freedori deck is to put as many Fire cards in it.

Example of a Freedori deck:

Ninjas:

Turn 0
1-Ino Yamanaka [Formation] (n-us013) x2
2-Sakura Haruno [A Double Personality] (n-us006) x2
3-Naruto Uzumaki [Legacy of the Fourth Hokage] x2

Turn 1
1-Sasuke Uchiha [Beyond the Limits] (n-155) x2
2-Temari [Wind Scythe] (n-us025) x2
3-Shikamaru Nara [Formation] (n-us014) x2

Turn 2
1-Neji Hyuga [Attack on Chakra Point] (n-095)

Turn 3
1-Hayate Gekko [Detecting a Plan] (n-122)

Turn 4
1-Kakashi Hatake [The Past in 10 Years Ago] (n-185)
2-Mikoto Uchiha [Motherly Love] (n-261)

Turn 5
1-Kakashi Hatake [Early Settlement] (n-064)
2-Kakashi Hatake [The Worst Outcome] (n-293)

Turn 6
1-The Third Hokage [Adressing Past Wrongs] (n-163)
2-The Third Hokage [Professor] (n-318)
Total Ninjas = 20

Platoons

Turn 5
1-Inochi Yamanaka & Ino Yamanaka [Combination Strategy] (n-us 050)
Total Platoons = 1

Missions

1-A Shadow in the Moonlight (m-us077)
2-Tide of the Deadly Combat (m-092) x2
3-Tsunade's Guess (m-272)
4-Just Like Drifting Clouds (m-us086)
Total Missions = 5

Jutsus

1-8 Triagram Divination Seal Spell Formula (j-006) x2
2-Sharingan Eye (j-007) x3
3-Lightning Blade Single Slash (j-281) x3
4-Lightning Blade (j-us066) x2
5- S. Action (j-234) x2
6-Chidori (j-211)
7-Chidori (j-131)
Total Jutsus = 14

POJO'S UNOFFICIAL TOTAL NARUTO!
This book is not sponsored, endorsed by, or otherwise affiliated with any of the companies or products featured in this book.
This is not an official publication.

71

WATER FLOOD DECK

**By: Nick Meisner
(2008 Stone Village Kage)**

The water decks in the Naruto Collectible Card game have one major theme: villainy! Most of the water cards seen in decks are the villains and bad guys in the Naruto universe. With that being said, you can safely assume that water has some of the meanest ninja and jutsu available, and that of course is correct.

Prior to **Lineage of Legends**, the Water element had major issues filling in its early game. Given, it had plenty of mid and late game ninja, but it severely lacked in early game ninja, making a mono-water deck rather hard to come by; many out of element ninja would have to be **"splashed."** However, with the set being released, water now remains competitive at major levels being able to hit its early turn drops.

Ranmaru (N-356) is a great turn zero ninja for water that protects your head ninja from effects that ninja like **Choji, Shikamaru, and Ino** posess to manipulate the abilities of your head ninja. Follow up with **N-055 Dosu Kinuta,** and you may only have two support, but a

team that can be nasty when blocked, giving 1 damage to their head ninja.

On turn two, you can drop someone like **Isaribii (N-384)** to get some draw power while blocking. This is also a great time to play **M-051, Appearance of Unknown Rivals** to fuel more draw power whenever your opponent plays a ninja. **Draw power** is the major weakness of water, so drawing cards whenever you can get them is perfect.

Around turn 3, you'll want to drop one of two ninja, either **Tayuya** (either turn 3 version), or if you prefer hand and chakra control, play **Princess Dusk (N-364)**.

Turn 4 leaves only one option for water, and that's **Aoi Rokusho(N-249)**. Turn 5 however is where Water really shines. Having ninja like **Zabuza, Kisame, Kabuto, Raiga and Kido** at its disposal, water really brings the heat. Any of these ninja would be great picks for turn 5, but I would not go over four turn 5 ninja in that slot. You don't want to make your deck too top heavy.

Turn 6 brings serious salvo in water, using ninja like **Kimmimaro, Orochimaru, and The Second Hokage. Again,** any of these ninja are exceedingly powerful, but don't use more than two for your turn six slot. **Orochimaru (N-353)** can pop off opponents ninja, and if you growth him in from another **Orochimaru,** you can avoid that nasty 2 hand cost. **Kimmimaro** can mess with your opponent's teams and lead you to an outstanding victory very easily. **The first Hokage** can either injure your opponent's ninja, or reduce their effectiveness in battle by decreasing their stats. The choice is up to you.

For the most part, water has staple jutsu, **Giant Vortex, Furious Current Jutsu, Hidden Mist Jutsu,** and **Senbon.** The other Jutsu will be determined by the turn 5 ninja that you use. With **Zabuza,** use damage Jutsu like **Water Shark Bomb. Kisame,** use **Chakra Burning Jutsu like Shark Skin. Kidomaru,** use his **Spider Bow: Fierce Rip. Water** is very versatile, and has the wonderful ability to mold to the player that uses it. Try a deck out for yourself.

Water Flood

Turn 0:
2x Ranmaru (N-356)
2x Naruto Uzumaki
(N-187, used for draw power)
3x Sakura Haruno (NUS-007, used to get a free mulligan)

Turn 1:
2x Dosu Kinuta (N-055)
2x Isaribii (N-384)

Turn 2:
2x Hisame (N-135)

Turn 3:
1x Tayuya (N-254)
2x Haku (NUS-035, used with Futaba for draw power)

Turn 4:
2x Aoi Rokusho (N-249)

Turn 5:
2x Zabuza Momochi (N-024)
2x Kidomaru (N-280, for combo with Zabuza, those two effects can instantly discard one ninja every turn.)

Turn 6:
2x Orochimaru (N-320)
1x The Second Hokage (N-369)

Mission:
3x Appearance of Unknown Rivals (M-051)
2x Selecting the Strongest (M-248)

Jutsu:
2x Water Style: Giant Vortex Jutsu (J-034)
2x Spider Bow: Fierce Rip (J-238)
1x Hidden Mist Jutsu (J-013)
2x Senbon (J-051)
3x Water Style: Furious Current Jutsu (J-332)

POJO'S UNOFFICIAL TOTAL NARUTO!
This book is not sponsored, endorsed by, or otherwise affiliated with any of the companies or products featured in this book.
This is not an official publication.

73

OVER 9000 DECK

By: Tom Yu
(2008 Sand Village Kage)

ey everyone. As the person that placed 4th at the Sannin 2008 tournament, I'm here to reveal my deck list and explain how it runs. This is a deck that is based around **Gaara [Immense Power]** and his sand jutsus, widely known as the **Over 9000 deck.** Gaara's ability allows the player to search the top 5 cards of their deck for a Gaara jutsu. This effect is the foundation for how this deck is built and played.

So in order for a deck that is based around one specific ninja to work,

you need to be able to draw him out. We have **Naruto, Sakura, and Kabuto** to help cycle through the deck. We have five turn-2 missions that allow the drawing of cards. This greatly helps with the chakra generation. These cards almost guarantee that Gaara will end up in your hand by turn 4.

Now that Gaara is out, it's time to gain field control. His jutsu searching ability ensures that the player will have more jutsus than their opponent, allowing the player to win the jutsu chain. Gaara acts as your main attacker but there are great ninjas to support him.

Among those include **Haku, Shikamaru & Temari Platoon. Baki and Tsunade** are great offense ninjas for late game once Gaara clears the field.

One card we need to mention in the deck is the client **Emi**. Her ability to stop a team allows Gaara's team to pass by and jutsu any potential threats such as **The Third Hokage [Addressing Past Wrongs]** or even another Gaara. This client even combos with **Baki**. This card, being near impossible to negate, should be added in all 9000 decks.

If you haven't tried this deck, give it a test run. It's a very good deck to run but it takes a bit of time before a player can master it. Keep working hard and try to obtain the title of Sannin.

Over 9000 Deck

Ninjas-24
3x Naruto Uzumaki [Legacy] N-187
3x Sakura Haruno [A Double Personality] N-US006
2x Choji Akimichi [US Formation] N-US016
3x Temari [Wind Scythe] N-US025
2x Shikamaru Nara [Flexibility] N-US015
1x Kabuto Yakushi [Information Sources] N-US074
1x Yashamaru [Sister's Memento] N-180
1x Haku [Camouflage] N-US035
2x Hayate Gekko [Detecting a Plan] N-122
3x Gaara of the Desert [Immense Power] N-295
1x Baki [Cleaning Up] N-130
2x Tsunade [Medical Expert] N-321

Platoons-2
2x Shikamaru Nara & Temari N-264

Jutsus-8
3x Sand Tomb J-270
3x Double Sand Blade J-288
1x Wind Scythe Jutsu J-054
1x Cyclone Scythe Jutsu J-250

Missions-5
3x Information Gathering M-263
2x Sakura's Decision M-080

Client-1
1x Emi C-026

POJO'S UNOFFICIAL TOTAL NARUTO!
This book is not sponsored, endorsed by, or otherwise affiliated with any of the companies or products featured in this book.
This is not an official publication.

75

Tournament Q&A

By: Eduardo "Beastly Mage" Miller

So, you're thinking of going to a tournament? Nice! But, you probably have a few questions in mind.

Q: Where are tournaments held?

A: Tournaments are usually held at **hobby & comic book shops** on certain days. Just ask the **Meijin** on times and dates. Also, special tournaments are held at Anime/Comic Book/Gaming conventions.

Q: Wait, what's a Meijin?

A: A **Meijin,** or Expert, is a **Bandai Games** volunteer. He or she can organize tournaments and judge over them. They're usually the owners of the shops, but they can also be just regular players.

Q: So, what do I need to play in a tournament?

A: All you need is a deck that's right for the kind of event being held.

Q: What sort of events are we talking about?

A: *There are many types of tournaments.*

__Constructed tournaments__ are just regular ones, with 40 card decks (no more than 25 Ninjas, and so on). They can be held at the shops or conventions. Any place with a Meijin supervising can hold an official tournament.

__Booster Draft tournaments__ are held at certain moments during the year, such as the release of a new card expansion. You don't need to bring a deck to this one, since you're going to build your deck right then and there.

Example of a Genin Pin.

__Rank tournaments__, such as Genin tournaments, are held every once in a while and the winners of such tournaments go up in rank (from Ninja Academy Student to Genin, for example). The winner gets a pin indicating what rank the player is currently in after winning. There is no Meijin Tournament if you're wondering since Meijin is a title and not a rank.

There are also special events, such as __Cosplay tournaments__ (which are kind of playing a tournament during a costume party), __Meijin Challenges__ (where the Meijin puts a special set of conditions to play), and others. Just talk to your Meijin.

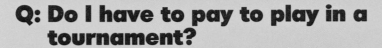

Example of a Prize Playmat

Q: Do I have to pay to play in a tournament?

A: *It all depends on what the Meijin decides. A tournament can be held for free, since the promotional material is free (if there is any). But, if prizes such as __booster packs__ and other things are involved, the Meijin can ask for an inscription fee.*

Q: Wait, I get something for free?

Example of a Prize Binder

A: *In most sanctioned tournaments you can get __promotional cards__. Also, winners may get such prizes as playmats and other things.*

Q: What else should I know?

A: *Remember to be a good player towards the Meijin and others. Don't __stall__ (that is, take too long in making just one move), follow the rules of the venue (where the tournament is being held), respect the other players, and (most importantly) have fun.*

POJO'S UNOFFICIAL TOTAL NARUTO!
This book is not sponsored, endorsed by, or otherwise affiliated with any of the companies or products featured in this book.
This is not an official publication.

77

TEN TIPS for COLLECTING and TRADING NARUTO CARDS

1. Above all else, make friends, be nice, and have **fun**!

2. Keep your cards either in **sleeves** or in a **binder** with special trading card sleeve pages. Cards for collections should go in a binder right away. Sleeves make cards in a deck last longer, and that means they should be in good enough shape for collecting later on.

3. Only trade when you can pay attention to trading. If you are playing and someone wants to trade, ask them to wait. It's rude to do both at once, and makes it easier to get cheated.

4. It's sad but true: some people make fake cards and try to sell them as the real deal. Easiest way to avoid getting ripped off is to only trade and buy from people you **know and trust**.

5. Price guides are useful, but don't just go by card name alone, as many cards are **reprinted**: remember that there are promo, foil, and other versions of cards that come out in packs.

6. The better a card is for **playing**, the more it is worth. Sometimes Commons are worth more than Regular Rares because of this!

7. Don't be fooled by a card being shiny. The easier a card is to get, the less it is worth. Some Super Rares can even be found in Starter Decks!

8. Keep your collection organized in a reasonable manner. "In order of favorites" isn't too helpful to someone else looking at your collection. But going by **"card number"** or **"set number"** can be, as well as rarity, card type, etc.

9. If you can afford it, buy a **whole box** at once! It is usually much cheaper than buying that many packs one at a time. It also makes it a little more likely you'll get the rarer cards in a set.

10. Go to some **tournaments** just to trade. Players trying to fix up their decks at the last minute will usually trade you more than normal for a card they really need.

TOP 10 CARDS: the PATH to HOKAGE (Series 1)

By: Eduardo "Beastly Mage" Miller

#1
Zabuza Momochi

[Demon of the Cloud Village]
n-024

Damage is good, and discarding is better in this game. Combine them both, and you have this guy. Make him your head Ninja and make your troubles disappaear.

#2
Konohamaru

[Hokage's Grandson]
n-007

This kid makes all of the Jonin, Sannin, and Satoosa Ninjas in your hand come out quicker in the game. What's not to love?

#3
Sharingan Eye
j-007

Simple, but effective. Negate and discard that Jutsu: true classic.

#4
8 Triagram Divination Seal Spell Formula
j-006

Return one Ninja to the top of your opponent's deck, and maybe even make that Ninja a Battle Reward in the process.

#5
One Morning
m-018

Draw two cards? Yes, please! A staple for Wind Decks everywhere.

#6
Bingo Book
m-011

Ninja search is good, and shuffling your deck can really help at times. Simple effect early in the game.

#7
Earth Style: Headhunter Jutsu
j-021

When you separate a Ninja from its team, you know that's trouble… for your opponent!

#8
Water Style: Giant Vortex Jutsu
j-034

Now this is a killer. Returning a whole team to the hand can sure hurt your opponent's whole strategy.

#9
Hidden Mist Jutsu
j-013

Jutsu negation is good, plain and simple. Even if it does return to the hand, it's still that good.

#10
Gato Transport
m-013

Chakra control is great. This card could just make your opponent think twice before going to battle.

TOP 10 CARDS! COILS of the SNAKE (series 2)

By: Eduardo "Beastly Mage" Miller

#1
Kakashi Hatake
[Early settlement]
n-064

This is one card that many fear. The ability to take battle rewards even when opposed is simply breathtaking to you, and painful for your opponent.

#2
Orochimaru
Reconnaissance
n-084

Having a Sannin-Level Ninja out on turn 3 could spell trouble for your opponent. With so many Jutsus at his disposal, the possibilities are endless.

#3
Wind Style: Great Breakthrough
j-079

Big price for a big, devastating effect. Just make sure this Jutsu goes through if you want to score that big win.

#7
Senbon
j-051

To heal? Or to pump up by a little? That is the question!

#4
The End of the Demon
m-052

Got a Water-Element Chunin (or higher rank) taking up space? Want to take care of someone on your opponent's side? Then this is the card for you.

#8
Sasuke Uchiha
[Analysis of Competence]
n-062

One of the best turn-zero Ninjas in the game. Just be careful with those pesky Jonin-rank Ninjas!

#5
Sakura's Decision
m-080

The card that made Kunoichi decks possible, and proves that smarts really are good.

#9
Paper Bomb
j-067

Damage? Make your opponent sweat a bit? Why not both?!

#6
Dosu Kinuta
[Sonic Impact]
n-055

When this guy is the head Ninja, your opponent may think twice before blocking.

#10
Disguise Jutsu
j-066

If you think Jutsu negation was good, you should take a crack at Jutsu protection. Make your Ninjas invincible for once!

TOP 10 CARDS! CURSE of the SAND [series 3]

By: Eduardo "Beastly Mage" Miller

#1
The Fourth Hokage
[Hero of the Village]
n-129

A card that truly belongs in Oil/ Toad and Lightning decks. Not just because of great stats, but also because of a game-saving effect.

#2
Baki
[Cleaning Up]
n-130

This Ninja's effect may prove devastating for your opponent. Getting rid of one Ninja is always good.

POJO'S UNOFFICIAL TOTAL NARUTO!
This book is not sponsored, endorsed by, or otherwise affiliated with any of the companies or products featured in this book.
This is not an official publication.

#3
Hayate Gekko
[Detecting a Plan]
n-122

This Ninja can fit well in many decks. Why? If Jutsu negation is good, then Mission negation is right up there with that.

#4
Wind Blade
j-123

Give one damage to a Ninja, and your opponent can't do anything about it. It's a great card for Wind decks.

#5
Wish
m-108

If played right, this card can not only restore your deck, but also stop Mill decks in their tracks.

#6
Neji Hyuga
[Attack on Chakra Point]
n-095

This is one of the reasons Neji is considered a genius. To stop a Ninja from using Jutsus is simply amazing.

#7
Ebisu
[Repeated Defeat]
n-121

Everyone's favorite loser teacher can help you draw, but watch out for those Satoosas. He'll just fall flat on his face.

#8
Tide of Deadly Combat
m-092

This card can really turn the tables on your opponent. You just have to play it at the right time.

#9
Lightning Blade
j-106

No matter how the coin falls, this Jutsu will always have a nice result... well, for you that is.

#10
Chakra Absorption Jutsu
j-095

Chakra control is always good. This card makes Water decks just a bit more powerful.

TOP 10 CARDS!
REVENGE and REBIRTH
(series 4)

By: Eduardo "Beastly Mage" Miller

#1
The Third Hokage
[Adressing Past Wrongs]
n-163

Even after the effect was corrected, this card is still good. A monster in Fire decks, and for good reason.

#2
Kabuto Yakushi
[Cover Operative]
n-152

Protection from targeting Jutsus is always good. A Ninja with that built-in effect, along with great stats is pretty close to perfect.

#3
Chidori
j-131

This is one killer Jutsu! It can potentially take out a whole team in one hit, and bring you one step closer to victory.

#7
Naruto 2K Uzumaki Barrage
j-145

Wimpy little Naruto can take out that big Ninja on your opponent's side if played right. Timing (and a bit of luck) will see to that.

#4
Orochimaru
[Eternal Youth and Life]
n-166

On top of great stats, an effect that can save him for later makes him a good choice for Orochimaru-based decks.

#8
The Second Hokage
[The Hokage Level]
n-168

Being able to reduce the cost of a Jutsu is an ability worthy of a Hokage. And, yes, some jutsus can be even used for free.

#5
Caged Bird
m-150

One of the best counter missions in the game. This card can stop that big hitter on your opponent's side for a while, and maybe even your opponent.

Secret Wood Style Jutsu: Deep Forrest Creation
j-159

#9

The First Hokage's top technique. To stop your opponent for a turn can give you the edge… and maybe even victory!

#6
Sasuke Uchiha
[Beyond the Limits]
n-155

The top card in Freedori decks. Being able to use a Jutsu for free (even if just once) is always a great effect.

#10
Naruto Uzumaki
[Control of Power]
n-136

One version of Naruto that's a good 0-drop. Pumping up a Ninja is worth it if you can fit it in your strategy.

POJO'S UNOFFICIAL TOTAL NARUTO!
This book is not sponsored, endorsed by, or otherwise affiliated with any of the companies or products featured in this book.
This is not an official publication.

87

TOP 10 CARDS: DREAM LEGACY (series 5)

By: Eduardo "Beastly Mage" Miller

#1
Orochimaru

[Deal]

n-217

Draw a card and give away a battle reward, or not draw and lose two cards… this card will make your opponent ponder on that.

#2
Kisame Hoshigaki

[Mysterious Man from the Hidden Mist Village]

n-202

The card that made Chakra control that good. Not only does he have great stats, but also has a great effect to take away whatever chakra your opponent may have.

#3
Toad Mouth Trap
j-175

Returning Ninjas to the hand has always been good in this game. Even if this is a coin-flip card, it's still that good.

#7
Dan
[Unrealized Dream]
n-210

Nice stats at turn 4, card drawing effect and a key card in many decks.

#4
Unfading Affection
m-201

A mission that makes the #3 card in our list tremble. Protect your Ninjas from removal with this card.

#8
Ninja Art: Mitotic Regeneration
j-202

Heal Tsunade, get a big hitter back on track, and get this Jutsu card back in your hand at the end all with one Wind Chakra. Very nice indeed.

#5
Fratricide
m-178

Got Ninjas you don't need any more? Send them to your Chakra area, and draw some cards while you're at it.

#9
Naruto Uzumaki
[Legacy of the Fourth Hokakge]
n-187

A card that has seen a lot of play lately. It allows you to draw even with growth (yes, I checked!). Just watch out for the Akatsuki

#6
Nawaki
[12th Birthday]
n-209

A key card in Jonin Intervention decks. Draw a card first, he goes out, draw a card again and maybe get a Jonin out of the whole deal…

#10
Water Style: Water Shark Bomb Jutsu
j-185

A Jutsu that saw a lot of play back in the day, but has since fallen to obscurity. Damage is good, no matter what sort of deck you play.

TOP 10 CARDS! ETERNAL RIVALRY (Series 6)

By: Eduardo "Beastly Mage" Miller

#1
Shikamaru Nara
[Flexibility]
n-us015

Mental power battles… from the smartest Ninja around. Just watch your hand, though.

Shikamaru Nara

Leaf | Genin | Male | Growth | Mental Power: 4

[FLEXIBILITY]
While you have 5 or more cards in your hand, this Ninja's Team and your opponent's Team Battling against this Ninja perform a Mental Power Battle. While you have 4 or less cards in your hand, this Ninja's Team and your opponent's Team Battling against this Ninja cannot perform a Mental Power Battle.

0/2

#2
Sakura Haruno
[A Double Personality]
n-us006

Another smart Ninja that helps. Change your hand at the right moment, and change the way the game is going for you.

Sakura Haruno

Leaf | Genin | Female | Growth | Mental Power: 3

[A DOUBLE PERSONALITY]
During the Exchange of Jutsu, you can exchange all the cards in your hand with the same amount of cards from the top of your Deck.

0/1

#3
Shikamaru Nara

[Formation]

n-us014 Yes, Shikamaru's twice on this list, and for good reason. This time he can negate the effect of your opponent's head Ninja AND reduce the turn cost to 0... OUCH!

#4
Temari

[Wind Scythe]

n-us025

A show of the hand to take care of one Jutsu is good, even if it does to go to the Chakra area.

#5
Gigantic Fan

j-us015

For one Wind Chakra you can negate a Jutsu with two or more specific symbols in its cost, which accounts for a lot of the big Jutsus going around.

#6
Shikamaru Nara & Asuma Sarutobi

[Shogi Match]

n-us040

A really big hitter combat and mental-wise, it will let you gain advantage by recovering the cards that went to the Battle Reward area.

#7
Jiraiya

[Instruction of the Hidden Technique]

n-us027

Jutsu recovery is one thing, and Jutsu recovery with great stats is a better thing. Remember: it's any Jutsu in your discard pile.

#8
Shino Aburame

[Tracking]

n-us011

Seeing what's in your opponent's deck and arranging it will probably delay that one card that can save your opponent for a while.

#9
Kakashi Hatake

[The Past in 10 Years Ago]

n-185

Giving growth to your Kakashis can be great in a Fire deck, particularly with so many good Kakashis around.

#10
Power of the Youth

m-us020

In the right deck, this is perfect. Attacking more than three times in a turn can really give you the victory quicker.

TOP 10 CARDS! QUEST for POWER [series 7]

By: Eduardo "Beastly Mage" Miller

#1
The First Hokage

[Great Founder of the Leaf]

n-us041

Being able to change the status of one Ninja with a turn cost of 4 or less is great, and can really stop your opponent at times.

#2
The Second Hokage

[Great Leader of the Leaf]

n-us042

Like his brother the First, he's able to change status. With great stats and his effect, he's a force to be reckoned with.

#3
Inochi Yamanaka & Ino Yamanaka

[Combination strategy]

n-us050

The best way to control the flow of the battle for many players. A great platoon card and an annoyance for your opponent.

#7
Aoi Rokusho

[Impeder]

n-249

Getting that Battle Reward back as Chakra is great. Just keep him protected.

#4
Itachi Uchiha

[Relentless Attack]

n-c008

The power to discard from your opponent's hand is great at times. With nice stats and Sharingan Eye, he can bring the hurt to the game.

#8
Haku

[Superhuman speed]

n-c007

Swarm potential is good. Add nice stats along with Mental Power and you've got a great addition for Water decks.

#5
Chidori
j-211

Not only does it boost either Kakashi or Sasuke, but it can also get you one more Battle Reward. That's one step closer to victory.

#9
Leaf Squad Organized

m-us030

Like the previous card, this brings swarm potential to the game. Imagine five Ninjas at once…

#6
Rasengan
j-210

To be able to pump up a Ninja is one thing, but to make a regular Victory an Outstanding Victory is just wrong… for your opponent, that is.

#10
Rasengan
j-us037

Like the previous Rasengan, it boosts power. But, this one damages a healthy stand-by Ninja. That's more pain for your opponent.

TOP 10 CARDS! BATTLE of DESTINY (Series 8)

By: Eduardo "Beastly Mage" Miller

#1
Gaara of the Desert
[Immense Power]
n-295

The main reason Gaara decks are popping up everywhere. Being able to search for his own Jutsus is simply amazing, as well as his stats.

#2
Kakashi Hatake
[The Worst Outcome]
n-293

With the usual Kakashi stats and an effect that allows you to recover Genin-level Ninjas, this is one Kakashi you may not want to overlook.

#3
Kimimaro
[The Most Powerful Pike]
n-279

If Kakashi [Early Settlement] was game breaking in the right deck by earning a Battle Reward per victory, imagine a Ninja that gives you that and a bit more.

#4
Shikamaru Nara & Temari
[Strong-Arm Tactics]
n-264

To be able to do or not to do Mental Power battles is great. With 5 Mental, some people actually worry about this card.

#5
Sasuke Uchiha
[Special Power]
n-289

With built-in protection against Ninja effects and Jutsu targeting, you'd think he wouldn't need such nice stats. In the right deck, however, he's fearsome.

#6
Naruto Uzumaki
[Special Power]
n-288

Clone Status, great stats, and protection effects... what's not to like about the one-tailed state?

#7
Jirobo
[Meal]
n-281

Chakra control at its finest, some say. Jirobo at State 2 can give you Chakra while taking it away from your opponent. A very nice effect.

#8
Kidomaru
[How to Beat the Game]
n-280

Even with a coin flip, he's a force to be reckoned with. Giving damage to any Ninja is simply fearsome in the right deck.

#9
Information Gathering
m-263

Three coin flips for the chance to draw three cards. Not bad, but not perfect. But, what card is?

#10
S. Action
J-234

Make that one Ninja go out in a blaze of glory... while taking another Ninja down too.

POJO'S UNOFFICIAL TOTAL NARUTO!
This book is not sponsored, endorsed by, or otherwise affiliated with any of the companies or products featured in this book.
This is not an official publication.

95

TOP 10 CARDS! the CHOSEN (series 9)

By: Eduardo "Beastly Mage" Miller

#1
Lightning Blade
j-us066

Turn Kakashi into a fearsome Ninja with this card by taking out Ninjas and maybe even boosting his power.

Lightning Blade

火 | 1

Requirements: "Kakashi Hatake"
Target: 1 Ninja Battling against the user
Effect: If your opponent has 5 or more Battle rewards, discard the target. If your opponent has 4 or less Battle rewards, give 1 Damage to the target. Additionally, the user gets +X/+X during this turn. X = the number of your opponent's Battle Rewards.

"By attacking one you infect all. And you don't care. That is not the way of the Shinobi."

術 us066 Ⅹ © 2002 MASASHI KISHIMOTO • • •

#2
Lightning Blade Single Slash
j-281

Make that whole team just go away with this Jutsu... and Kakashi himself.

Lightning Blade Single Slash

火 火 | 1

Requirements: "Kakashi Hatake"
Target: Every Ninja Battling against the user
Effect: Give 1 Damage to the target.

"You can't beat me..."

術 281 Ⅹ © 2002 MASASHI KISHIMOTO

#3
Kakashi Hatake
[Gifted Ninja of the Leaf Village]
n-316

A Kakashi with Mental Power: 3?! Plus a drawing effect?! For some that's crazy, but in the right deck it's simply beautiful.

#4
The Third Hokage
[Professor]
n-318

One of the potentially strongest versions of the Third. Just watch your Chakra pile if you want to keep him that way.

#5
Orochimaru
[Master of Every Jutsu]
n-320

To be able to use pretty much every Water Jutsu in the game regardless of requirements will bring a headache to your opponent.

#6
Naruto Uzumaki & Sasuke Uchiha
[Explosion of the Ultimate Jutsu]
n-us066

Great stats in healthy and injured forms, plus the ability to reduce Jutsu costs. Not for every deck, but great for its own.

#7
Naruto Uzumaki & Neji Hyuga
[The Genius and the Knucklehead]
n-us068

This platoon's effect can really save the day in many situations. To either recover Battle Rewards as Chakra OR to draw two cards… simply genius.

#8
A Shadow in the Moonlight
m-us077

If you thought Bingo Book (m-011) was good, then take a crack at this card.

#9
Hinata in Captivity
m-283

Stopping your opponent from earning battle rewards is great, even if for a few turns. Although this card can be negated, the price for that is a bit high for your opponent.

#10
Hinata Hyuga
[Overcoming the Weakness]
n-330

A potential powerhouse, this Hinata can go from mousy to monster in a few turns.

TOP 10 CARDS! LINEAGE of the LEGENDS (series 10)

By: Eduardo "Beastly Mage" Miller

#1
The Fourth Hokage
[Lightning speed]
n-371

This guy rocks! Getting an extra battle reward is good, but getting past a chump blocker is even better when the time is right.

#2
The Fifth Hokage
[Establishment of Medicine]
n-372

Free healing is always good. And, with monster stats like hers, you have a real powerhouse to consider.

#3
Jiraiya

[Eccentric Man of the Village]n-352

Hand control just found a new friend in Jiraiya. Remember, you can get past the double hand cost with Growth.

#4
Orochimaru

[Lurking Evil]
n-353

If you liked Baki (n-130), then you'll love this version of Orochimaru. He's also "Leaf", which makes him even more interesting.

#5
Tsunade

[Unrivaled Strength]
n-354

Could she work in a Mill Deck? Maybe, but, trust me, losing four cards in one hit is not pretty… for your opponent, that is!

#6
Princess Dusk

[Wandering Ghost]
n-364

If played right, Chakra control could become Hand control. Try it and see!

#7
The First Hokage

[Secret Wood Style Jutsu]
n-368

This Ninja could become quite pesky for your opponent… or just delay the inevitable. Remember to play him right.

#8
The Second Hokage

[Water Style Jutsu]
n-369

Not only can he weaken your opponent's Ninja, but he can help you recover Chakra. A great addition for Water decks.

#9
Raiga Kurosuki

[Funeral of the Living]
n-355

A great addition to Chakra control's arsenal. Just remember to keep him protected.

#10
Emina

c-035

Mill's worst enemy! To recover cards is great, and to draw a card is simply life-saving at times.

POJO'S UNOFFICIAL TOTAL NARUTO!
This book is not sponsored, endorsed by, or otherwise affiliated with any of the companies or products featured in this book.
This is not an official publication.

99

TOP 10 CARDS! PROMO CARDS

By: Eduardo "Beastly Mage" Miller

#1
Naruto vs Sasuke
pr018

This card is just crazy. It can bring a victory quickly in the right deck.

#2
Gaara of the Desert

[Tragic Name]
prus008

The Ninja is at the center of several great combo decks!

#3
The First Hokage
[The One Who Created the Village]
pr018

A life-saving effect for many. Discarding your opponent's Battle Rewards is simply that good.

#4
The Second Hokage
[The One Who Established the Foundation]
pr019

Card drawing is great. In Water decks, he's pretty good.

#5
Kakashi Hatake
[Sharingan Eye Kakashi]
pr009

A strange effect, some say, but quite effective back in the day.

#6
Naruto Uzumaki
[One Last Attack]
prus011

He gets damage, an opposing Ninja gets damage… plus it's valid!

#7
Big Boss
prus006

To stop Chakra payment effects is great in the right deck, even if the art is a bit disgusting.

#8
Sakura Haruno
[I Can Do It]
prus010

Mental Power battles have always been good. If you can find a way to use her effect right, it's a victory for you.

#9
Naruto Uzumaki
[Unlimited Potential]
pr014

More than one Growth coin on this Ninja means more power for him… and for you.

#10
Successors
pr011

In the right deck, this promo card can give you the winning edge.

POJO'S UNOFFICIAL TOTAL NARUTO!
This book is not sponsored, endorsed by, or otherwise affiliated with any of the companies or products featured in this book.
This is not an official publication.

101

GEN CON INDY

Gen Con Indy is the original, longest running, best attended gaming convention in the world.

By: Pojo

People having been going to Gen Con to play games and have fun since 1968. In 2008, more than **27,000** people attended Gen Con Indy!

The convention takes place in a large exhibit hall in Indianapolis in August, and runs for four days (Thursday through Sunday). The convention is filled with game publishers, artists, and related gaming businesses.

People go to Gen Con to play Collectible Card Games, Board Games, War Games, Live Role-Playing Games, Computer Games & more. You can also **play test** dozens and dozens of games you've probably never heard of. Many gaming companies show up at Gen Con to unveil new games. Other gaming companies are there to tease you, and show you future expansions

that will be available for the holiday season. Still other gaming companies make rare miniatures and trading cards for sale only at Gen Con.

The World Championships of many games are held at Gen Con.

Many people go to Gen Con to dress up in their favorite costumes. On Saturday, there is a huge Costume Contest. Naruto characters are usually well represented by the costumers.

Bandai usually has nice presence at Gen Con. They have a demo booth where folks can learn to play the Naruto Collectible Card Game (CCG), and win some free stuff. This year they were giving away free packs Naruto Trading Cards, Naruto figurines, Naruto Playmats, and more. Bandai was also demonstrating their new Dragon Ball Z CCG that plays just like Naruto. If you don't know how

to play the Naruto CCG yet, the Bandai Naruto booth is a great place to learn. Experienced players are there all four days teaching people how the play the Naruto CCG.

Bandai also runs several huge Naruto Tournaments. This year they had several fun tourneys like: "3 v 3" tournaments; the "Forest of Death Exams" tournament; and the "Sannin" tournament. The "Sannin" tournament is essentially the Naruto CCG World Championships. In the "Sannin" tourney, folks can win laptop computers, Xboxs, PSPs, Nintendo DSs, iPods and more.

Another great thing to do at Gen Con is shop. You can buy games, gaming accessories, shirts, dice, miniatures, artwork, and more from the many vendors at Gen Con. We found some rare Naruto phone charms, Naruto headbands, Make Out Paradise leather notebooks, Kunai Knives, Naruto T-shirts and more. Of course we bought quite a bit for ourselves!

We hope to see you at Gen Con next year!

Phone Charms

HEY! Get those Pokemon cards OUT A HERE!

NARUTO WORD SEARCH!

Find all your favorite Naruto characters in this Ninja Word search!

Search the puzzle on the opposite page and circle all of the characters listed below.

ASUMA	CHOJI	GAARA
GUY	HAKU	HINATA
INO	IRUKA	JIRAIYA
KAKASHI	KANKURO	KIBA
KONOHAMARU	KURENAI	LEE
MIGHT	NARUTO	NEJI
OROCHIMARU	ROCK	SAKURA
SASUKE	SHIKAMARU	SHINO
TEMARI	TENTEN	TUSNADE
ZABUZA		

Find all your puzzle answers at: www.pojo.com/naruto/answers.shtml

Naruto Character Search

```
D O F Q F E R H I U N G S F U
X H R G R L C I S R I W C R A
S S F U A J J N Z A A J A D S
S V H I K I B A O G K M E E U
O H B I R N B T A H I U E N M
G E I A N U A A U H K N R T A
F U I K Z O I K C K A L A A H
P Y Y A A C H O J I K R K C O
A L E E K M R C I S A S U K E
R V K B U O A V P A S J N X R
I I A N E R U K R G U H W F U
N N E T N E T L H U K I M K B T
L J Z R C R T T D A V A I U H
I Q W G L V A X M H T K R F G
U U N P G N D N I Y F A R F I
K O N O H A M A R U N N N J G M
```

NARUTO "HIDDEN MESSAGE" WORD SEARCH

Naruto Villains • Hidden Message Word search

Find all Naruto's villains. **A hidden message will be revealed from the letters you do not use.**
These villains made a tough puzzle for you!

As you look for the hidden words, remember that they can be horizontal, vertical, or diagonal—frontward or backward! Some letters may be used more than once.

Be like Naruto, and Never Give Up!

BAIU	DEIDARA	DOSU
GATOU	HAKU	HIDAN
JIROBO	KABUTO	KAGARI
KAKUZU	KIDOMARU	KIMIMARO
KISAME	KONAN	MADARA
MIDARE	MUBI	OBORO
OROCHIMARU	SAKON	SASORI
SHIGURE	TAYUYA	UKON
YOROI	ZABUZA	ZAKU

Naruto Villains Search

```
D O F Q F E R H I U N G S F U E
X H R G R L C I S R I W C R A D
S S F U A J J N Z A A J A D S A
S V H I K I B A O G K M E E U N
O H B I R N B T A H I U E N M S
G E I A N U A A U H K N R T A U
F U I K Z O I K C K A L A A H T
P Y Y A A C H O J I K R K C O R
A L E E K M R C I S A S U K E I
R V K B U O A V P A S J N X R N
I A N E R U K R G U H W F U A O
N E T N E T L H U K I M K B T I
L J Z R C R T T D A V A I U H Q
I Q W G L V A X M H T K R F G K
U U N P G D N I Y F A R F I U
K O N O H A M A R U N N J G M F
```

Leftover Letter Hidden Message?

" __ __ __ __ __ __ __ __ __ __ __ __ __ __ __

__ __ __ __ __ __ __ __!"

– Naruto Uzumaki

NARUTO CROSSWORD PUZZLE

Across

5 – "If I were you, I'd let Akamuru go."

6 – "I planted a beetle on you as you left the arena … a female beetle."

9 – "Itachi chose me to be the avenger of the clan!"

10 – "I find this clan hopefully unfit for my capacity."

11 – "I need to control my Chakra with more precision to find small things like insects."

12 – "Special tip for you. I can radiate my chakra from any chakra points on my body."

13 – "If I can't attack my opponent 100 times while he's falling, I'll do 200 push-ups!"

15 – "These classes are such a drag."

17 – "Please … please bring back Sasuke … "

Down

1 – "A Ninja's talent lies in the use and master of every Jutsu that exists in this world."

2 – "Sorry I'm late, I got lost on the road of life"

3 – "I'll give you the answer! I am a sage associated with toad spirits from Mt. Myoboku and therefore generally known as 'Toad Sage!!'"

4 – "The pleasure of this last piece of meat is allowed only to me."

5 – "You haven't seen half of what Crow can do. So far he's been playing nice!"

7 – "I don't quit and I don't run!"

8 – "I want to prove you can become a splendid ninja even if you can't use Ninjutsu or Genjutsu!"

14 – "Desk work isn't really my thing!"

16 – "I'm not a fool but you are. It's nothing for me to create the sand under the ground."

They Said It
Crossword Puzzle

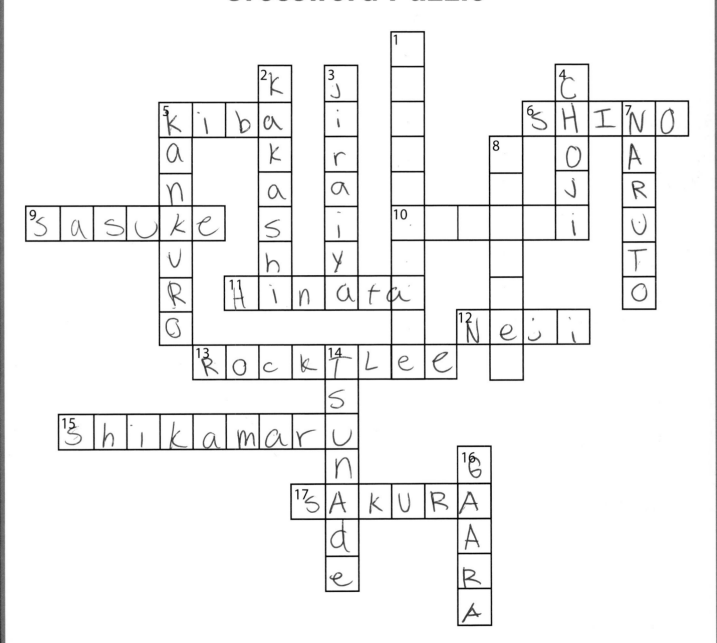

Use Each Ninja only once.

Naruto – Sasuke – Sakura – Shikamaru – Rock Lee – Jiraiya – Kankuro – Kiba – Shino – Choji –
Itachi – Orochimaru – Tsunade – Gaara – Neji – Might Guy – Hinata – Kakashi

POJO'S UNOFFICIAL TOTAL NARUTO!
This book is not sponsored, endorsed by, or otherwise affiliated with any of the companies or products featured in this book.
This is not an official publication.

111

NARUTO MATCH

Match the Village Symbols to the Village Names. Draw a line from the Village name to the Village symbol.

See like a TRUE Ninja!

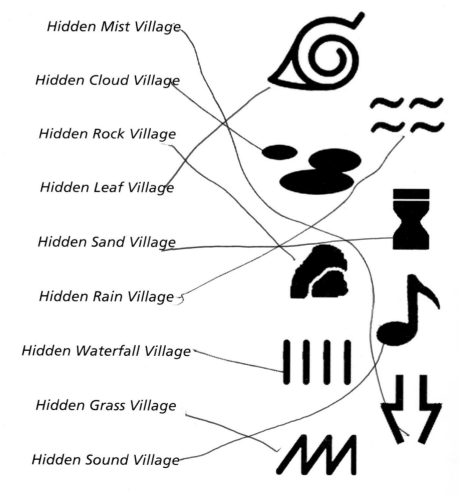

Hidden Mist Village

Hidden Cloud Village

Hidden Rock Village

Hidden Leaf Village

Hidden Sand Village

Hidden Rain Village

Hidden Waterfall Village

Hidden Grass Village

Hidden Sound Village